The
Christmas
Remedy

Books by Cindy Woodsmall

As the Tide Comes In

The Amish of Summer Grove series

Ties That Bind
Fraying at the Edge
Gathering the Threads

Sisters of the Quilt series

When the Heart Cries
When the Morning Comes
When the Soul Mends

Ada's House series

The Hope of Refuge
The Bridge of Peace
The Harvest of Grace

Amish Vines and Orchards series

A Season for Tending
The Winnowing Season
For Every Season
Seasons of Tomorrow

Novellas

The Sound of Sleigh Bells
The Christmas Singing
The Dawn of Christmas
The Scent of Cherry Blossoms
Amish Christmas at North Star
The Angel of Forest Hill

Nonfiction

*Plain Wisdom: An Invitation into an Amish Home and
the Hearts of Two Women*

The Christmas Remedy

An Amish
Christmas Romance

CINDY WOODSMALL

Best-Selling Author of *The Angel of Forest Hill*

& ERIN WOODSMALL

WATERBROOK

THE CHRISTMAS REMEDY

The characters and events in this book are fictional, and any resemblance to actual persons or events is coincidental.

Hardcover ISBN 978-0-7352-9104-1
eBook ISBN 978-0-7352-9105-8

Published in the United States by WaterBrook, an imprint of the Crown Publishing Group, a division of Penguin Random House LLC, New York.

WATERBROOK® and its deer colophon are registered trademarks of Penguin Random House LLC.

Library of Congress Cataloging-in-Publication Data
Names: Woodsmall, Cindy, author. | Woodsmall, Erin, author.
Title: The Christmas remedy : an Amish Christmas romance / Cindy Woodsmall and Erin Woodsmall.
Description: First edition. | Colorado Springs : WaterBrook, 2018.
Identifiers: LCCN 2018014003| ISBN 9780735291041 (hardcover : alk. paper) | ISBN 9780735291058 (ebook)
Subjects: LCSH: Christmas stories. | BISAC: FICTION / Christian / Romance. | GSAFD: Love stories. | Romantic suspense fiction.
Classification: LCC PS3623.O678 C56 2018 | DDC 813/.6—dc23
LC record available at https://lccn.loc.gov/2018014003

Printed in the United States of America
2018—First Edition

10 9 8 7 6 5 4 3 2 1

To Adam Woodsmall
(Cindy's son and Erin's husband)

You took a leap of faith to attend pharmacy school
and became the first doctoral graduate in the family.
You inspired the best traits of the caring pharmacists in this story,
and your diligence to treat every patient with respect and care
encourages those around you to strive to be better people.
Thank you for all your help.
Without your knowledge of pharmacy law and practice,
this story wouldn't exist.

1

*H*olly paused outside the old pharmacy storefront, brass key in hand. How could a building be so dear to her? Because inside the brick, glass, and wood exterior, the beautiful, timeworn store held the hope that medicine brought to her Amish community.

She slid the key into the antique lock and jiggled it. The wooden door that Lyle had painted red last year had a hundred years' worth of paint on it. It creaked as she went inside, closed it, and turned the dead bolt. The customary smell that reminded her of an attic in summertime filled her senses. She unbuttoned her sweater and walked across the rough-hewn wooden floors.

"Hey, kiddo," Lyle greeted her from his workstation—a counter that was two feet above the rest of the pharmacy. His black with silver hair was somewhat disheveled, and his reading glasses had slid down the bridge of his nose. His focus was on whatever prescription he was filling.

"Good morning." She went up the three steps and waited for him to push a button under the counter of his workstation. The familiar buzz let her know the gate had unlocked, and she entered the area where all the prescription medicines were housed—the prescription workstation as they called it. There were a few odds and ends for her to do here, and then she could make her morning deliveries. She'd be back in a couple of hours, by the time the pharmacy opened at ten. "How are you today? Ready to start the week?" She stepped into the storage room and pulled out two large plastic bags, one with amber vials and one with white lids. Before leaving for the weekend, she'd noticed that the pharmacy bins were running low. She carried the bags to the counter next to Lyle.

He closed his eyes and rubbed his temples. "It's a very Mondayish Monday."

"What's going on?" She opened the bags of vials and lids and dumped each into its own bin.

"Nothing too bad. I have a wicked headache, but I'll take some Motrin after I eat my breakfast. I'll be right as rain by the time we open." Lyle held up a white prescription bag from his perch. He waggled the bag and put it in the bin that held the morning's deliveries. "Don't worry about me. With the health fair this weekend, you've already got a ton of work to do after these deliveries are made."

A smile tugged at her lips at the mention of the health fair. She'd worked for more than a year toward this goal—first getting unanimous permission from the Amish church leaders to hold the fair and then getting her people interested in attending.

Based on recent feedback and people signing up for classes, the health fair was going to have a fantastic turnout. Hope for the fair and her future stirred anew. After years of her proving her faithfulness to the bishop, deacon, and preacher, they had agreed to let her get her GED. She had accomplished that a year ago, and since then they'd approved her continuing her studies. If she could pass the entrance exam for nursing school, she could become an LPN. She personally had no grand desire to have a degree, but legally she had to be an LPN in order to verbally share the information written on the Patient Package Inserts. Until she had her LPN license, every patient question had to go through Lyle. She wasn't allowed even to read from or reword the information on the insert. Besides, with a license she could then offer some basic health care to Amish patients in their homes, especially the ones who often refused to venture out to the *Englisch* doctors and clinics.

Until that time she had to content herself with routine tasks, like refilling the two printers with paper—a roll of prescription labels in one and letter-size paper in the other. She grabbed the needed supplies and went to the first printer.

She turned to Lyle. "Are the morning deliveries ready?"

"Almost." Lyle looked back and forth between his computer screen and the pill in his hand. He put the pill into its bottle, closed the lid, slid it into a prescription bag, and stapled it shut. He set the bag in the delivery bin.

She pulled an index card out of the hidden pocket in her apron and took a moment to study it. *Granulocytes respond quickly to infectious agents. Define granulocytes.* She knew the answer to this one. It was a white blood cell with granules that secreted its cytoplasm. But how tough would it be to pass the test to get into nursing school?

"Holly Noelle, before I forget, I have something for you."

"Hmm?" She tucked the card back into her pocket.

Lyle reached under the counter and behind a large paper bag. He pulled out a beautiful bouquet of pink carnations in a cut-glass vase and set them on the marred glass countertop. A familiar ache she'd never be free of caused memories to crash in on her. She touched the petals. They were just as soft as she remembered. She leaned in and drew a deep breath before opening the envelope of the small note card nestled in the bouquet.

With Sympathy –

She lifted a carnation from its glass container. "You remembered."

Her *Daed* used to give her a pink carnation on special occasions, usually when she'd worked hard toward something and accomplished it. She'd been fourteen the last time he'd given her one, in celebration of her months of spending endless hours in his cramped office space, which was overrun with paperwork. She'd finally gotten his dairy farming business affairs in order, including years of receipts for tax purposes. A week later he died.

"Thank you." Her hoarse voice was hardly more than a whisper.

"Sure thing, kiddo," Lyle said. "I know it'll be an emotional day for you. Hard to believe he's been gone ten years. And even though I don't mark his passing each year, I never forget. You just let me know if you need to take a break or to shift some of your deliveries to another day."

Holly swallowed the lump in her throat. "No, I want to work. Today of all days." She set the card inside the bouquet and moved the flowers to the far side of the cash register. She picked up the bag Lyle had just put in the delivery bin and read the insert—name, address, and medicine. "This is a new medication. He'll have questions."

"I know."

She returned the bag to its bin. "*Ya,* you know, but the question is whether you'll be where you can hear the phone when I call."

He chuckled. "That is always the question, isn't it?" He tapped out something on the keyboard of his computer, verifying another aspect of the dispensing process. Lyle never rushed through the correct process for ensuring that every client got the right medication and that the new prescription wouldn't be dangerous in combination with other medications the patient already took. "Be done in a minute, and when I am, I'm going upstairs to shower and eat. And take something for this headache."

"Okay." She knew the routine, but he always stated it anyway.

She checked the list of meds and addresses. Each year they were making a greater difference in the lives of the Amish. They were pushing past indifference and lack of understanding. She hated those descriptions of her people. As a whole they were passionate and sharp but not when it came to medical issues and taking the medicines that had been prescribed. But Lyle, Doc Jules, and Holly had spent years trying to make inroads. Her people were responding—but slowly, because the Old Ways of ignoring health issues and discounting the importance of medicine were a way of life just as surely as traveling by horse and carriage. So the road ahead was long, but the Amish in this rural area weren't where they used to be. For that she was grateful.

Indifference and ignorance had stolen her Daed's life, and there hadn't been a more passionate, intelligent man in Raysburg. What a horrendous waste. If he'd gone to the doctor sooner . . . If he'd then valued the doctor's advice and taken his medication . . .

Now she had to miss out on a whole lifetime with him.

Closing her eyes against the onslaught of the invading grief, she tried to refocus on her task. She opened her eyes and finished mentally mapping her way between the addresses on the delivery list. "That's quite a list of deliveries for today."

"It is. I'm not sure you'll be back here by opening time, which is fine. So I'm telling you now, if that happens, relax and breathe."

Not be back on time? She glanced through the addresses, thinking of the shortcuts she could take in the carriage on dirt roads. "I think I can do it."

"Only if I finish checking these scripts off, right?" Lyle studied another pill in his hand and glanced at the computer screen.

She chuckled. "Right."

"While I finish here, could you flip through my morning to-do stack of papers? I think I needed to call someone first thing today, but I don't recall the specifics. This headache is really messing with my routine."

"Sure." She laid down the list of addresses to deliver to and retrieved Lyle's always-growing stack of papers in the bin next to his workstation. "Was this it—'call to confirm tent rentals for Saturday'?"

"No, I did that already. I believe it was for a patient that came in yesterday."

"Oh, hmm." She flipped through a few papers and saw an offer from a security company for a remote-controlled surveillance camera. They had the mandatory ones inside the store that monitored everything that took place behind the pharmacy counter. But after someone broke into an independent pharmacy in a small town a few hours away, Doc Jules had suggested Lyle look into surveillance of the entryways and the store itself. She resumed digging through the stack until bright red writing on a document caught her eye: "Past Due. $45,640. Redbird Pharmaceutical Distribution."

Her heart jolted. A past-due notice on a bill that large? She shouldn't ask about it. It wasn't her store, and he wasn't family, even though he often felt like it, but . . .

"Lyle . . . what's this?" She handed him the paper.

He took it from her and peered down at it through his reading glasses. "Oh, that's from our medicine supplier, and I have that already set up to pay online on a specific date. It'll only be a week late once paid, and there's no penalty."

"But . . . that's so much money. Do we have that kind of money? I know things have been tight after a slow summer."

"We will by later in the week. It's just part of the business, kiddo. It's why this place is open seven days a week."

"I thought you stayed open on Sundays to help people."

"Well, that's true. But I also need their business. We're doing fine. Trust me."

She wanted to trust him, but he might hide the truth in an attempt to protect her. Finances were usually tight after the quieter summer months, and since the financial downturn a few years back and subsequent law changes, the pharmacy wasn't making nearly what it used to.

Lyle set the paper down and moved back to filling the script.

Could Greene's stay open in the long term? Lyle was nearing retirement age, and if he had to shoulder this much responsibility every month, even with Adrienne as a relief pharmacist, he might choose to retire before finding a replacement. But the Amish people needed this place, and that wasn't going to change.

"There you go." He placed another bottle in a white paper bag and then put that bag in the plastic bin Holly used for deliveries. "After I eat and shower, I might be in and out between now and opening time. I have a few calls to make and some errands to run."

She picked up the bin. The new thought of the pharmacy's uncertain future swirled together with her grief over missing her Daed, but she had deliveries to make. Chin up. Put a smile on. "Okay. See you around ten."

2

*J*oshua moved supplies from the horse-drawn wagon to the baby chicken nursery. He strode back and forth, trying to make quick work of the process. He had no time to lose. This old shed-type building hadn't housed chicks in two years and never this late in the season. Had he made the right decision to take on these birds in October? "Labor intensive" didn't begin to describe what the first two weeks with newly hatched chicks were like.

"How are you doing, Son?" His Daed carried in a box of warming bulbs. His white hair and beard reminded Joshua of unmarred winter snow. For being almost seventy, Daed was sturdy, but he couldn't tend to this farm on his own anymore, especially with *Mamm's* new diagnosis. Diabetes wasn't rare, but it was a fresh burden.

"I'm good." Joshua had already set out four large metal bins made especially for chicks. He was doing all he could for his Mamm's health, but for now he had to focus on something he could control, and that was keeping these chicks alive. While his older brothers and sisters nursed and tended to their baby humans, he was here, still living at home and preparing for baby chickens. And with the way things went between him and the only girl he'd actually liked, he might always be here tending chicks instead of elsewhere with newborns. He pushed those thoughts aside, determined not to start thinking of her again. He had no doubts she didn't think about him. "I'm better now that you've found the last item on my list."

Daed set the box on a high shelf next to the other warming lamps. "You look stressed."

"I'm feeling the pressure. A hundred hatchlings arriving between eleven and noon?" He didn't need to explain to his Daed that when the chicks arrived, they would not have had a bit of water or food since hatching yesterday. Joshua and his Daed would have to deal with each one individually, giving them water and then food. If he and his Daed didn't handle them with quick finesse, some would become too weak to swallow by midafternoon. "I'll get everything set up in time." He hoped.

When the hatchery he'd always ordered his birds from called him, asking if he'd take a hundred hatchlings, he was sorely tempted to say no. He never would have ordered chicks for his free-range farm this late in the season. Young ones often didn't fare well in Pennsylvania winters, even in a heated barn, but someone had ordered a hundred Easter Egger chickens, and then two days before they were hatched, the person canceled the order. Without a home all would die from lack of attention, or they would be killed so they wouldn't suffer.

He put fresh heat bulbs in the four brooder lamps and went out the nursery door and around the building to check on the gas-powered generator. Besides the fact that the chick nursery wasn't ready to receive them, Joshua had two additional strikes against him in this venture. He'd never raised young ones this close to cold weather, and he'd never raised Easter Eggers, period. He wasn't sure how many he could keep alive until spring, but he had to try.

The gauge on the propane tank indicated it was half-full. He'd order more this afternoon, but this was plenty for the next few weeks. On his way back from the generator, he stopped at the wagon and grabbed a large box of old newspapers and a crate of cedar shavings. His Daed was standing there, looking confused, and his brows were creased. Was he worried about Mamm? It'd been a tough weekend for all of them, but she was home now, resting. Or was he concerned about the chicks that were arriving?

"Daed." Joshua set the newspapers and crate of cedar shavings on the floor. "Don't let anything worry you. We'll take good care of Mamm and the chicks, I promise." Joshua grabbed a stack of newspapers. "Besides, these birds lay colored eggs. Can you imagine what a huge seller that will be at Easter? Free-range, naturally colored Easter eggs." He passed the newspapers to his Daed.

"True." His Daed took the hint and began spreading newspapers in the metal bins. "I hadn't considered that part."

Joshua nodded. "You're having a hard time considering much of anything right now except worrying about Mamm. But you have to trust me. I'll see to it that everything runs smoothly—Mamm's doctor's visits, her meds, and the farm." He didn't feel as confident as he sounded, but his Daed needed to be reassured.

"You know, Son, ten years ago when you wanted to change to free-range and expand this business, I never would've expected it to take off like it has."

His Daed had said that same thing to him on numerous occasions, maybe because ten years ago he had balked at the idea when Joshua wanted to tear down the battery cages and convert the farm to free-range. "You feel bad for not believing me sooner, but looking back, I can't believe you trusted a teenager about any business ideas." Truth was, Joshua grew up hating to see chickens cooped up in a tiny space. It just seemed wrong to treat God's creatures like that, and he'd told his Daed so numerous times over the years. Then at fifteen he stood his ground, making his

Daed hear him. They'd argued for weeks, but his Daed came around to seeing Joshua's point. "Free-range chickens have proved to be a worthy investment, ya?"

The Smucker family's free-range chicken farm had been experiencing a surge in popularity at the farmers' markets recently as many people—Amish and Englisch alike—were paying more attention to humane farming practices, to his Daed's delight and Joshua's reserved liking. He was definitely glad that the farm was doing better financially. However, a higher demand for eggs meant more work for him, the only one of the thirteen siblings who still lived at home.

His Daed continued lining the floor with newspaper. "I'm surprised you found all this stuff in storage."

"Me too. I thought I might have to buy more than just the chick starter feed when I go to town. Oh, before I forget, I called several drivers earlier and found one who was willing to take me to Raysburg to that Greene's Pharmacy the doctor told us about. He should be here a few hours after the chicks arrive, so I'll get them squared away, make a quick trip to the pharmacy, and come back to nurture them some more."

"I just can't see making your Mamm give herself a shot of that stuff every single day." Daed shuddered. "Surely there are other things we can do for her."

"Not according to the doctors at the hospital. Or the clinic doctor that gave us a second opinion. It's not just a temporary 'spell,' as she's been claiming from time to time for years. She has diabetes. I don't like it either. But we're not gambling with her health, so we do what the doctors say. Every time."

"None of you kids ever needed to take any of these expensive medicines that so many Englisch are on, and neither did your Mamm and I."

Joshua shrugged. "We avoided having to go this route for as long as possible, but this weekend was scary. I never want to see her faint like that again and end up in the hospital. The docs say we have no choice but to get her on a specific medicine, and I believe them. So let's not have this conversation again, okay?" He didn't want to argue with his father, certainly not today when he had so much to get done.

His Daed sighed. "You ready to take care of these little fluff balls?"

Good. Daed was changing the subject. Joshua secured the extension cord to the wall and snaked it around to connect to the warming lamps. "Yeah. I'm not thrilled about the tedious tending the chickens will need when they get themselves all pasty. But it'll be worth it come springtime when they are laying pretty colored eggs that fetch extra money at the markets around Easter."

"I'll share the chicken diaper duty with you. Don't worry. I've never been afraid to get dirty. Knew that when I went into this business."

Joshua had just begun sprinkling the shavings over the papers when he heard car tires on the gravel driveway. He looked at his Daed. "Isn't it too early for the shipment?"

"Unless that's your driver."

"Good grief, I hope not."

They stepped out of the shed, crossed the free-range field, and headed toward the driveway. Joshua shut the gate behind them, keeping his current chickens contained.

A familiar-looking man maybe in his forties got out of a red car. "Is this Smucker Farm?"

"Yes, I'm Albert Smucker." Daed approached the man, hand held out.

"I'm Chad Richards, manager of Real and Fresh, a grocery store."

He shook Daed's hand. "I spoke with a Joshua Smucker at the farmers' market a few weeks ago."

Suddenly it clicked, and Joshua could place where he'd met the man. "That's right. Hi." Joshua moved next to his Daed and offered the man his hand. "Chad is opening a grocery store about an hour from here, Daed, and he's using all local items that are available. He was looking into carrying our eggs."

"I like the sound of that." Daed gestured toward the henhouse. "You want to come meet our birds? My son and I would love to show you around."

Chad glanced at the old battery cage building. "I'm sure you both know this, but in order to be called free-range according to the law, the chickens can have as little as a few minutes a day outside. I won't accept that, let alone anything less. I wanted to come by to make sure your farm went beyond that, you know?"

"Sure. See those battery cages?" Joshua pointed. "They haven't been used in more than a decade. We use that building for storage now. I think you'll be pleased with our flock and their houses." Joshua motioned to the wide, picturesque farmland with chickens visible behind the fences. "I can give you pictures to take with you to show your customers as well. Want to take a walk?" He had time. He could show this man around and still finish setting up the brooding pens before his driver arrived.

"That'd be nice."

As Joshua let Chad through the gate to where the chickens roamed, he heard another car in the driveway. *No way.* He turned. Well, the good news was that the baby chicks hadn't arrived. The bad news was that his driver, Fred, had.

"My dad will walk with you. Excuse me for a minute." He really wanted to show Chad around himself. Joshua had made the contact, and his Daed's mind wasn't as clear as usual right now, but at the same time Joshua *needed* to get his Mamm's medicine.

Fred beeped the horn and rolled down his window. "My plans changed for the day. If you need to go to Raysburg, it's now or not today."

Joshua couldn't go by horse and buggy. It was too hard on a horse to travel there and back in one day, and it'd take the whole day to do it. "We agreed—"

"I know that, but you said it had to be today, and I have right now. Actually, I have one hour to get you there and back, which gives you exactly seven minutes to get the prescription and get back in my car before I have to go. Unless you can wait until later this week."

"No. Let me give my guest a quick goodbye."

His Daed would have to handle this grocery store manager on his own. Joshua had to get to the pharmacy. His Mamm was more important than any amount of chickens, eggs, or money.

3

*H*olly breathed in the crisp morning air, admiring the splendor of the hills wearing their best October colors. The air smelled a little of fall but also hinted at the promise of a long Indian summer. Her Daed had loved fall. Even now she could see his grin as the beauty of this season awed him year after year.

Her phone sounded a familiar *ping,* reminding her that the store would open in thirty minutes. She clicked her tongue, encouraging Stevie to pick up his pace. Lyle had been right. She might not get back in time to open the pharmacy at ten. That would be a first. "We're almost at the last stop, boy. I've got a yummy apple for you."

Stevie's ears perked at the word *apple,* but the white horse continued on faithfully without answering. Holly smiled. She was used to their one-sided conversations.

The beauty of the morning and the pleasure of talking to customers had caused the deliveries to go smoothly, except a few people hadn't been able to pay the full amount for their medicines. Was that why Lyle needed to keep the store open seven days a week—to make up for the losses because he gave the poorer Amish people as much of a break as he could?

Stevie's hooves clip-clopped down the dirt road, kicking up dust. *Clip-clop, clip-clop, clip-clop.* "Lyle thinks I should hire a driver, and schedulewise I agree. But being a girl and having my newfangled, highly suspect medicines, I wouldn't be as welcomed if we did that."

Stevie snorted, nodding his head.

"Ya, you're right. You'd be lonely without this, wouldn't you, old boy?"

Again Stevie didn't answer.

Finally arriving at her last destination, she pulled on the reins to stop Stevie, hopped out of the rig, and tied him to the hitching post. Like every other Amish family Holly knew, John and Ruth Troyer had a hitching post for guests. She paused and rubbed Stevie's fuzzy white face. Then she gave him his promised apple.

The old farmhouse with its aging pale-blue paint had seen better days, much like the elderly couple who'd lived here for almost fifty years.

"Be right back, Stevie boy." She gave him a final pat and reached into her rig to grab the bag of prescription medications she was delivering. The house truly begged for a fresh coat of paint, and she wondered if she could convince her brother and a few of his friends to take that on as a charity project.

She knocked on the front door, and after just a few seconds it opened.

"*Guder Marye,* John." Holly grinned. The old man didn't know it, but he was one of her favorite customers.

"Holly Noelle! Whenever you visit, it's like an early Christmas." The older gentleman chuckled as he held the door for her.

"Care for some coffee, *liewi*?" Ruth held up a percolator.

"*Nee, denki.* You two are very kind. I wish I could stay longer, but I'll have to head out soon." She needed to keep moving, although she would have liked to stay for a while and enjoy this fun couple.

Ruth set the percolator back on the gas stove. "How's your family these days?"

Holly discreetly checked the time on her phone while Ruth was turned away. She'd need to wrap up this visit in a few minutes if she was going to make it to work on time. "Mamm and Ivy are still cleaning houses since we don't have the hands to run much of a dairy farm at this time. Red is courting a girl—Emily over in Rocks Mill—and working for a painting company while he's there. Mamm has mentioned wanting to catch up with you soon, and I'm sure she would tell you much more about my little brother and his girl. Unfortunately, the pharmacy opens soon, and I need to get back. Speaking of . . ." She handed the bag of prescriptions to John.

"Denki. Our Holly Noelle came bearing gifts."

"Ya, but it's not really Christmas, so they aren't free." She winked at Ruth. "Do you have any questions?" Not that she could legally give an answer, but she was required to ask that question, and giving them an answer is where contacting Lyle by phone became a part of these visits.

John emptied the bag onto a side table, picked up a pair of reading glasses, and carefully examined the labels on the three bottles. "I'm not sure about this one. It must be the new med the doctor wanted me to start. Any side effects?" He handed the bottle back to Holly.

She read the label: furosemide. The tablet was a common heart medication that she helped dispense almost every day. She wanted to ramble off the side effects that she knew: it can make you more sensitive to sunlight; it can make you urinate frequently and lose weight. If you have sudden weight gain, you need to go to the hospital. But she had to hold her tongue.

"I'll get Lyle on the phone. Hopefully, it'll just take a moment."

"Take your time." John sat down in his recliner.

Ruth joined him in the living room. Holly paced the creaky wooden floor while pressing the cell phone against her ear. She'd begun working at the local pharmacy with Lyle Greene ten years ago and started carrying a cell phone not too long afterward, but each time she used her iPhone, the irony of her plain Amish appearance in contrast to the new technology was not lost on her. No answer. She tried the main line at the pharmacy. Still no answer. But the pharmacy wasn't officially open yet, so Lyle could be running errands. After reaching Lyle's cell phone voice mail yet again, she moved the phone away from her ear and ended the call.

She tucked an escaped strand of hair behind her ear and slid her phone into the hidden pocket of her black apron. "I'll have to come back later today." If she was the least bit passive about anyone getting or taking the proper medication, she would easily undo her years of effort.

John put his shaky hands on the armrests of his chair and pushed until he was standing. "Denki, Holly Noelle. I'm sorry you have to make another trip, but I don't know what Ruthie and I would do without you and Mr. Lyle."

"Ya." She set the medication on the table beside him. "I know what you'd do. You wouldn't take your medications." Holly tapped the lid of the bottle. "I'll be back this afternoon, and we'll get your questions answered."

"Here you go." John shook her hand, putting cash in her palm as he did.

"Denki."

Holly hoped he'd given her the full amount on the receipt, but she'd count it later. Lyle often sold medication at cost, no profit involved. But at sixty-five years old, he would eventually have to retire and sell the store, hopefully to another pharmacist who cared about her people. It would be even harder to find that kind of pharmacist if Greene's Pharmacy didn't turn a decent profit. Maybe she was looking too far down the road, but if the pharmacy ever closed its doors, how would she continue moving her people to take better care of themselves? There were big pharmacies five or so miles away, right off the closest highway, but horses and carriages couldn't go on highways. So the pharmacies might as well be a hundred miles away as far as most Amish were concerned. The sharp rise in costs for doctors' visits and medication was enough of a deterrent for her people, and that would only increase in the coming years. They didn't need the added issue of having to hire a driver to get to a pharmacy.

Holly thanked them both again and waved as she exited their front door.

Stevie snorted at her as if to say hello. Or maybe he was asking for another apple.

"Kumm." She patted his head. "How about some fresh oats at the lot?" Once she was in the carriage and headed back to Raysburg, Stevie knew where he was going. She held the reins in one hand and with the other flipped through the list of Amish families that had agreed to come to the health fair she, Lyle, and Doc Jules were planning. Perhaps she could pop in the office for a quick chat with Doc Jules after she spoke with the Troyers again.

The horse clipped along, and she kept one eye on the road and a firm hand on the reins while studying the list. There weren't enough hours in the day to focus on just one task at a time.

Soon Stevie came to his usual stop—the small pasture next to the Martel Clinic, where Doc Jules worked. A few other horses were already inside the fenced space, standing at the feeder under the lean-to, their owners most likely at the office or at a local shop. After tying off his reins, she gave him his oats and then crossed the street and walked along the sidewalk toward the downtown pharmacy.

Store lights peered through plate-glass windows, greeting her with a soft hello each morning she worked. She wrapped her sweater tighter around her and hurried up the sidewalk. As she approached Greene's, she noticed an Amish man peering into the front window. He stood up straight and looked down the block. He appeared to be about her age and had no beard. Between her vision jostling as she hurried his way and his moving every few seconds, she couldn't see his face, but he was tall, blond, and fit. Very fit.

"Isn't it unlocked?" She glanced at the town clock. Fifteen minutes after ten. Did Lyle forget to open the door? She lengthened her strides and dug into her apron pocket for her key.

The man turned to face her squarely.

Oh no. No. No. No. Of all the people . . .

Memories of Josh Smucker—though most called him Joshua—filled her mind, and he stared at her, speechless. She'd gone with Ivy to a singles event in another district. That's when she met him, and it was about this time last year. They'd enjoyed six months of playful camaraderie during the socials after singings and at singles functions—volleyball games, bonfire gatherings, hayrides. She'd kept him at arm's length, sharing very little about herself while enjoying the fun activities. She'd fooled herself into thinking it was just a lighthearted, acquaintance-type friendship.

Then he'd asked her out.

Taken aback at his question, she'd stood in front of him, gazing into his beautiful brown eyes, and realized just how deeply attracted to him she was. It'd been all she could do not to flee to the carriage right then and hightail it out of there in terror. Instead she'd stammered her way through what she'd hoped was a polite decline and vowed to herself never to attend another singles event—at least not one he might be at. Since his district was so far from hers, she'd simply bowed out of his life. Until now.

What was he doing this far from home?

He finally broke the silence. "*You* work here?" The scowl on his face detracted very little from his natural good looks.

"Ya." *Just breathe, Holly.* She put the key in the old lock and jiggled it.

"But I thought . . ." He sighed. "Never mind. It doesn't matter."

The key didn't turn. Antiques were nice, but some things needed to be updated. Like locks. Would Josh be less irritated if she told him the truth—that she would not let anything or anyone prevent her from reconstructing how her people dealt with their health? She would stay the course. Save lives. Renew minds that would continue to impact generations of people long after she was gone. Amish women had to give up all work outside the home in order to marry, and after a woman was wed, babies started coming, often a newborn every two to three years until age began to reduce her fertility. She could barely keep up with the pharmacy and education needs as a single woman. Not that he'd necessarily had marriage in mind. If he'd had the chance to really get to know her, he probably would've chosen to extract himself from her life. Few men could tolerate a headstrong woman.

What was wrong with this lock? She lifted the doorknob and tugged on the door while putting pressure on the key.

When she was honest with herself, she found the whole headstrong thing a bit frustrating too. Sometimes it was as if her will had a will of its own. Nevertheless, she'd increased awareness about following through on taking prescribed medicines and, in so doing, had saved a few families from losing a loved one. A couple of years ago she even prevented her Amish friend from ignoring all medical advice when diagnosed with intrahepatic cholestasis of pregnancy. Holly's determination might have saved the mom's and the baby's lives and definitely saved them from a lifetime of health struggles.

Why wouldn't the key just work already? "Mr. Greene must be running a few minutes behind."

"Seems to me he's not the only one."

"No." She kept her voice pleasant. *Stupid lock.* "I'm not late. I deliver medicine to people." The lock finally turned, and she opened the door. "Come on in." She whooshed inside and gestured for him to enter, holding the door for him and trying to respond to him as she would anyone else. The lights in the pharmacy were on, and the pharmacy window was open. Apparently the only thing Lyle had forgotten was unlocking the door to the storefront.

Josh walked inside and stopped in front of her. "This is really annoying." His brown eyes bore into hers. "The doctor lady said this was the best place to come. That you people would get me all set up in short order to tend to my Mamm's illness, and yet I've been waiting for fifteen minutes." He glanced down the block. "I'm not even sure my driver is still here."

This was Josh. Honest as the Pennsylvania winters were long. He wasn't a people pleaser, and it was part of what she'd liked about him. In a society where manners were equal to salvation, he offered no pretense whatsoever.

"Doctor lady?" She closed the door behind them and walked across the store at a quick pace.

He followed close behind. "Julie Wilson."

"Ah."

Julie wasn't technically a doctor, but most Amish referred to her as one, herself included, just as they called Lyle, Doc Lyle. Holly forced her voice into the default cheeriness she used for all her customers. "I'm sorry we've slowed your morning. I'll do my best to get you on your way."

"Of course you will."

She turned around. Her eyes snapped onto him, and she longed to defend herself. But men didn't understand what it was like for an Amish woman with a career calling. Actually, men didn't believe in such a thing. A woman's calling was to find a husband, serve him well, and populate the earth with obedient, well-behaved offspring. Thanks, but no. She was trembling all over as she broke eye contact and walked behind the counter. "Your name?"

He moved to the register. "Seriously?" His tone was somewhere between disbelief and anger.

She refused to react to him. *Chin up, smile on.* She forced a smile, hoping it looked more genuine than it felt. "Sorry. I meant to ask for the name the prescription is under."

"Edith Smucker."

Did she know Edith Smucker? Truth be told, she shouldn't know Josh, but thanks to Ivy and her idea to venture a little farther outside their district, Holly ended up at a new singles event before she realized what she'd agreed to. Still, it wasn't anyone's fault but her own that she returned to the singles events in Josh's area time after time. "Okay, I'll get it." She craned her neck and stood on her tiptoes. "Lyle?" She went up the small set of steps that led to Lyle's workstation. "Lyle?"

As she looked in, she could see his feet sticking out from between two rows of shelves and pointing toward the ceiling. *Dear God, no!* Her heart stopped. Ten years ago she'd stumbled upon her Daed, and his feet had been pointing skyward too.

Move! He needs help! But she just stood there. She pulled her attention from his feet to look at the rest of him. Lyle was sprawled on the floor, eyes closed.

"Something wrong?" Josh's voice seemed to be lost inside a canyon, echoing.

Answer him! But no words would form.

"What's going on?" Josh squeezed next to her and peered over the gate. "We need to call 911." He jiggled the gate, trying to open it, but only Lyle had the keys to that.

Her body refused to move, seeming more frozen than her mind.

"Kumm on, Holly." Josh clapped his hands. "He needs you."

Lyle needed her? Her people needed him. Josh yelled her name again, but her brain was processing slowly, as if she were hearing the words underwater. She drew a shaky breath, finally able to think.

She jumped down the small set of steps she had climbed earlier and shoved the black pharmacy phone across the counter toward Josh. "You call." She ran up and flung herself over the gate, folding her body at her waist and kicking her legs until her hands were on the landing. She pulled the rest of herself over and rushed to her boss. She pressed her fingers into his neck, checking for a pulse.

Dear God, please don't let him die!

4

*B*randon closed his eyes and rubbed his temples. Blood pounded, and the nerves in his head felt like guitar strings that had been pulled too tight, probably from his staring too long at the most boring book in the world. When his dad was trying to pass his boards all those years back, had he studied anything as tedious or hard to memorize as *Pennsylvania Pharmacy Law: A Complete Study Guide*?

Delicate hands setting a mug of steaming coffee in front of him caught his attention. "You look exhausted. And it's only ten in the morning." Mila tapped on the closed book. "Need help studying?"

He picked up the mug and sipped the fragrant, dark liquid. If she could hand him his state license and a promotion to pharmacist along with the coffee, his headache might ease.

"Brandon Greene." Mila had cupped her hands around her mouth. "Hello?"

He pushed the weight of his failures to the side. "Oh, hi." He held up the mug and smiled. "Thanks."

"What is going on with you lately?" Mila flopped onto his well-worn paisley-print couch and sprawled out. She pressed buttons on her phone, seemingly scrolling and texting.

Did she even need to ask that question? She should know the truth. He attracted misfortune like a magnet drew metal.

She probably wanted another assurance that he was fine. But she

knew the real score. He'd failed an internship round because his preceptor lied, counting him as late when the preceptor had been the one who
was late. How could a lowly intern whose parents weren't rich straighten
out a mess like that? The only way to fix the issue had been to retake the
internship round, which he'd done. But the mess had knocked him off
schedule, and he hadn't graduated with his class.

He looked around his apartment, noting how out of place she seemed
inside this dump. The rented apartment he shared with two roommates
matched its seventies' decor, and the wear and tear made each item look
as if it was almost ready for the garbage heap. Mila had her own place,
a nice one, and she had her PharmD. What a powerful term: *PharmD.*
She was officially a doctor of pharmacy. She also had a job and, oh, no
student debt. They were polar opposites in these areas, but all he needed
was one tiny break—his license—and then the pharmacist job would
surely come.

Her question hung in the air, and eventually she put down her
phone. "What happened stinks. All of us know that, Bran. But maybe
you need to push harder. See if the administration will make an exception
for you and let you graduate now. You've finished every requirement, just
like all the rest of us who've graduated."

"I did. There's no budge anywhere."

"I'd be beating down the dean's door or something."

"I've been to see him twice. The appeal process for late graduation
applications can be heard only at a full school board meeting, and the
next meeting isn't until November. So there's no point. I can't take the
NAPLEX or MPJE until after that."

"This is just crazy. You were *making* the study guides for all of us back in the first year, and I've been a pharmacist for almost three months now."

Her words were flippant, but he knew her, and she didn't mean to come across that way. On days like today he would willingly give up a pinkie finger if it meant he could suddenly have his license. He tossed the book onto the floor, and it landed with a thud. "Good thing one of us has money, right?" He winked, trying to steady his rising blood pressure. "Look, our preceptors are just given way too much power. He declared I was the one who was late when he actually was, and there is nothing we can do about—"

"Are you sure you weren't actually late?" Mila sat upright. "Like sure, sure? I mean, I could understand your telling everyone else that excuse so you wouldn't feel embarrassed, but you can tell me the truth."

Even *she* didn't believe him? "I thought you just said everyone agreed that what happened to me stinks?"

"They do think that. Me too. I just . . . was wondering out loud, I guess."

"Good grief. What motivation would I have to lie?" Brandon stood and picked the book off the floor. "It's not like lying would change the outcome. It was my word against his, so of course they went with him. Like I've said before, I was late once. I didn't lie about that. I wasn't late the second time."

"And it's two strikes and you're out, I know."

The question kept repeating in his head—she didn't believe him? "So how long have you doubted that I'm telling you the truth?"

"I don't know. It's just that sometimes, like watching you today, it feels as if you're floundering."

"While the rest of the graduating class have their careers on track." He tossed the book onto the kitchen table.

"I wanted to do something fun today, and there's never time or money for that."

"I don't even know where to start in an argument like this. You have no idea how it feels to struggle with money."

She made a dismissive sound. "You think that school was easy because I didn't need to take out student loans? Money issues didn't cause the preceptor issue, and besides that, your father is a business owner and in pharmacy, no less. It's not like you were bad off."

"Yeah, but he put everything he made *back* into the pharmacy." Brandon would never understand why the Amish were more important to his dad than his own son, but he tried to accept it with as little rancor as he could manage. "I know I'm swimming up to my neck in student loans, and nothing has gone right for a while." That was an understatement. He'd been dealing with setbacks for a long time, but within three months he'd have his license and be able to move up from his current position as a graduate intern to a pharmacist with BB Drugs. Thankfully he didn't need to have graduated to be a grad intern. He only needed to have successfully completed all classes and rotations. His workday was the same as the pharmacist on duty, except an intern couldn't do the final check on prescriptions, and pharmacists made a good wage. A manager pharmacist made even more.

BB Drugs was a huge franchise, and he hoped to quickly work his way up to management. But even if he didn't get a promotion to manager, he'd be making enough money to pay his student loans *and* eventually buy a house, a modest one.

Mila studied him, arms folded.

He smiled. "You're right. We haven't done anything fun in way too long." He sat next to her on the couch and moved in closer. He kissed her lightly on the lips. "How about if we go to . . ." He angled his head, thinking, teasing, ready for this argument to end.

"Yes." Mila licked her lips and drew a deep breath, already looking happier.

He laughed. "I haven't come up with an idea yet."

"Anywhere fun will do, Bran. I'm not hard to please. I just want time with you."

There was a hiking trail to a waterfall about an hour away. "How about—" His phone rang, and Brandon pulled it from his pocket. A name he rarely encountered flashed across the screen: Holly Zook.

"Don't you dare answer." Mila raised an index finger, and he knew she was sort of teasing, and yet if he answered, they'd argue again.

"I have to. It's Holly Noelle, my dad's lead tech. She never calls me." He slid his finger across the bar icon to answer the call.

5

$\mathcal{H}$olly paced the length of the ER waiting room for probably the two hundredth time. The air seemed thick, as if there wasn't enough oxygen to fully satisfy her body. Her heart continued to race, and her hands were still shaking. Waiting was torture. But she wasn't a relative, so she couldn't get any more information until Brandon arrived. To make matters harder, this hospital didn't allow nonrelatives to enter ER until a relative gave permission. A relative would arrive shortly . . . she hoped.

The call to him was the worst she'd ever had to make. While riding in the front seat of the ambulance, she'd had to raise her voice over the chaos to break the awful news to Brandon: his dad had most likely had a stroke.

No one would tell her anything, and if the doctors needed permission to do a procedure on Lyle, she couldn't give it to them. Why did the law have to assume a blood relative was more involved and loved the patient more than the people who spent time with the patient? She owed Lyle so very much, and all she could do for the man was pace the floors and wait for Brandon to arrive.

After finding her Daed on the floor of his office, feet facing skyward, she had scrambled to the phone shanty and called for an ambulance. He had died of sepsis four days later. It'd been preventable, so completely preventable.

Stop.

She redirected her thoughts. Lyle and his wife, Beverly, took her under their wings, giving her a much-needed job at fourteen years old. They paid her two dollars above minimum wage—a mere child who needed more assistance from them than she'd provided to them, but that money kept food on her family's table. Four years later Beverly died, and Holly did her best to help Lyle get through that time. He moved out of the big house where he and Beverly had raised Brandon. Holly helped make the living quarters above Greene's Pharmacy as homey as possible. She had cooked for him, worked beside him, and kept him company while Brandon remained in his last year of college before he entered pharmacy school. Now, six years after his mom's death, Brandon was graduated from pharmacy school and still never found much time to visit his dad. Truth was, she should have more rights over Lyle's welfare than Brandon, but the law didn't see it that way.

She glanced up from staring at the white-and-gray dotted tiles. The few other people in the waiting area seemed similarly encumbered. No one chose to hang out in a hospital for fun. Why wasn't Brandon here by now? She could call him again, although that would do no good. Calling him wouldn't make the miles between him and the hospital disappear. She checked the time on her phone again.

"Holly!"

She looked up to see a younger version of Lyle hurrying toward her. *Finally.*

Brandon had the same hazel eyes and black hair as his dad, but Lyle's hair was now salt-and-pepper gray.

She went to him. "I don't know anything more than what I told you on the phone."

He took a deep breath. "Yeah, I know. I just spoke to a nurse. He did have a small stroke, but he's stabilized and doing well, considering. She said they moved him into an ICU room a few minutes ago. Come on. Let's go find him."

Minutes later a nurse led them into a hospital room. Lyle was reclined in the bed.

He opened one eye. "Took you two long enough."

Holly couldn't find her voice. The left side of his face drooped, and she rarely saw him reclining even in a chair, but other than that he looked a lot like his usual self. A huge wave of pure relief washed over her.

He lifted a finger off the bed and wagged it from her to Brandon. "Now which one of you is going to open the pharmacy?"

"Um . . ." Holly didn't quite know what he was asking them to do. She didn't have the legal authority to open the pharmacy. Had Brandon passed his boards? Holly tried to catch Brandon's eye. "Do you have your license?"

He glanced at her but didn't answer. "Good to see you too, Dad. I think the pharmacy needs to be the least of your concerns right now. But just so you know, I already called Adrienne, and she's there now. I haven't been able to reach Harris yet, but he has Tuesday down as an available day to work, so he should be able to cover tomorrow's shift."

Adrienne was the relief pharmacist who worked every Thursday and Saturday to give Lyle a couple of days off each week, and Harris was a fill-in pharmacist for Greene's, but his full-time job was working for BB Drugs. A couple of years ago the big company had given Harris permission to take any extra hours Lyle offered. Harris worked two jobs in hopes of saving enough money to open his own store one day.

Lyle waved his hand dismissively. "The Amish patient I'm expecting to see today after church needs a Greene there."

Holly's heart pounded. His words were slurred and a little hard to make out, but he thought today was Sunday?

"It's an emergency fill," he continued. "It took a while to build that kind of trust, and we have to honor it."

Brandon frowned. "Dad, it's Monday."

"Monday?" Lyle's eyes narrowed, as if he thought Brandon was lying to him. Lyle focused on Holly.

She grabbed his hand and squeezed. "It's Monday. When I came in this morning, you had flowers for me, and we talked about what today is, remember?"

His eyes watered as he shook his head. "No. So did the man get his prescriptions yesterday?"

"What man, Dad?"

"I . . . I can't remember." He closed his eyes, his face taut as if he was concentrating. "Did I lose a whole day? Or a week? Did I miss the health fair?" He sounded as if he was speaking to himself.

Health fair? That wasn't until this weekend. And did he expect them to be at the pharmacy during a time like this?

Holly held his hand tight. "The health fair isn't until this Saturday."

"Okay." He rubbed his head. "I filled a prescription for three members of the Frank Thomas family on Saturday, and . . ." He rattled off some of the highlights of Saturday's accomplishments, grounding out each word as if arguing with someone.

Holly grinned. "Ya, that's right."

"But today's Monday?"

She nodded.

"Did the doctors tell you what happened?" Brandon's voice was calm and measured, sounding a lot like his dad did when he addressed his patients.

"I don't need them to tell me what happened." Lyle spat a curse word. "I had a stroke. I take good care of myself. I do everything I tell my patients to do. Yet I'm lying here, useless at sixty-five."

Holly wanted to say *you aren't useless,* but she moved to a window, fighting to keep her emotions under control. Tears kept trying to overwhelm her. In all her time of knowing Lyle, he'd never cursed, raised his voice, or sounded so confused.

"Irritability is a common symptom after a stroke and concussion." Brandon held a small tissue over her shoulder. "Personality changes come with the territory. Just take it in stride. It isn't personal."

She took the tissue and forced the right words. "Okay, thanks."

Brandon returned to the bedside. "Dad, just try to relax. I promise it'll—"

A gentle knock interrupted him, and a female doctor entered. She was probably in her forties, and she had pixie-cut brown hair.

"Mr. Greene, I'm Dr. Davis. How are you feeling?" She smiled warmly as if they were meeting under happier circumstances.

"Take a wild guess."

"Well, I'd say ill tempered, which is a good sign actually. But we need to talk about a few things, and I can't guess at the answers, okay?" She smiled at Brandon and then Holly. "I need to ask you to leave, so if you'll excuse—"

"This is my family. Whatever you need to tell me, I consent to have them in the room."

She nodded. "What we're dealing with here is known as an ischemic stroke. You also suffered a concussion when you fell. We caught both pretty quickly, so we are feeling optimistic about your prognosis. I'm going to give you a quick exam and ask you a few questions. Just answer as well as you can."

Holly stayed near the window, watching as the woman asked a series of what seemed like random questions in pretty quick succession. At one point she drew a clock on her clipboard and asked Lyle to read her the time. After she was done, she made a few notes on her tablet.

"I'll be back to check on you soon. In the meantime if you need anything, please page the nurses using this call button." She smiled as she exited the room.

Had the doctor told them anything helpful about Lyle's condition?

Lyle turned to his son. "So did I pass?"

Brandon grimaced before looking out the window. "Let's just speak with the doctor when she comes back."

"Come on. I felt like I got 'em all."

"It was an MMSE. You scored a fourteen."

Lyle rolled his eyes. "It's been a while since school. Is that good or bad?"

"It appears your brain isn't functioning at its usual level. But it could be worse. Please, try to give yourself a break. You just had a stroke."

Lyle muttered another curse word. "Guess I'm not getting out of this one easily." He glanced at Holly, seeming to realize anew that she was in the room. "Sorry about the language, Holly Noelle. Thank you for being here."

A tear escaped and rolled down the side of her face. "I wish I knew what to do to help."

"Start by getting me out of here. I can't stay in this hospital. We'll figure it out from there."

Brandon's eyes met hers, and it was clear he shared her concern. Lyle was undoubtedly not acting like his normal self. What would the path look like from here?

"Dad, don't put that on Holly. Your doctors will be the ones best able to determine your care. If you will recover faster by staying in the hospital for a while, then that is what needs to happen." Brandon rested his hand on his dad's shoulder.

A tense silence enveloped the room. Holly needed to say something, anything, to reassure Lyle, but no words came. Not for him or herself. The clock on the wall seemed stuck. It made the right noise, a faint *tick-tock,* and the bright red second hand moved, but time seemed heavy and slow.

There was a knock on the door. Maybe more time had passed than she realized. Was it the doctor?

Harris stuck his head in the room. His short blond hair had looked the same every day since Holly met him five years ago, except now he was graying at the temples. "May I come in?"

"Yes, come on." Lyle waved a hand to gesture him in. "We're waiting for the doctor to return with test results. Could be a while. You know how these things go."

Harris walked to Lyle's bedside. "You look good, although I'm not sure what I was expecting when I got here."

"You were expecting to see a man who's seen better days. And that's me." Lyle gestured to his asymmetrical drooping face.

"I'm sorry this happened." Harris put a hand on Lyle's shoulder. "Are you comfortable sharing what you know so far?"

"Yeah, but Brandon can tell you."

Brandon quickly filled in Harris with the information the doctors had given them earlier. No matter how many times Holly heard it, the event still felt surreal.

"Sounds like the doctors have the situation under control. I apologize for intruding here at the hospital, but I needed to see you with my own eyes. I worked a morning shift at BB Drugs and got Brandon's message when my shift was over. I've canceled my golf plans for today. Whatever you need, name it. Think Adrienne could use a hand?" He glanced from Lyle to Holly to Brandon, looking uncertain as to who could answer his question.

Holly nodded. "I'm sure she could. Medical emergency or not, it's still a busy Monday, after all, and she has to be behind since the store was closed until Adrienne could get there."

Lyle crossed his arms. "I told these two to get over there and work, but they wouldn't listen."

"Then I'll go right now, so ease your mind about it. Just leave the pharmacy to Adrienne and me. We'll get caught up in short order. Brandon, you'll update me when the doctor tells you more?"

"Of course."

Harris moved to Holly. "No worrying, not about Lyle or the pharmacy. Promise me."

She nodded, and he gave her a firm but quick hug before saying goodbye to all of them and exiting the hospital room.

A few minutes later another gentle tap sounded on the door as it swooshed open, and the doctor who had been here earlier reentered. "All right, Mr. Greene. I think we can come up with a plan to get you out of here quickly and yet make sure you are recovering and safe. We need to keep you a few days for observation. This is standard after an ischemic event. Based on the head CT we did, we don't think you need a stent or surgery. We're going to give you more medicine to thin your blood. We need to make sure that there's no pressure on your brain and that any clots are broken up. After that you'll be released to go home to the care of your family. You will need someone there with you."

The doctor glanced at Holly a few times, looking a little confused, maybe because of Holly's Amish attire, but she didn't ask. No doubt she saw Amish regularly. They lived in Pennsylvania. But it had to be uncommon for the woman to see an Amish person beside an Englisch patient like this, as if Holly were related to Lyle. The doctor turned her full attention to Brandon. "After his necessary time here, if there isn't someone who can stay with him, he could be moved to a rehabilitation center for a few weeks."

"Be here a few days? Then elsewhere for a few weeks? No way."

"Lyle." Holly used her best parental tone. "You dispense advice with medicine all the time. Now take advice without arguing. If someone within the Amish community knew you didn't take your doctor's advice, that balking could undo years of hard work."

Lyle rolled his eyes again and sighed. "Fine. I'll stay."

Holly kissed his cheek and wiped off the spot. "Denki."

"I'm *not* going to a rehab facility after this."

No one responded to him, and the doctor continued to discuss with him the medications and the type of things they would be checking for while he remained in the hospital. Holly and Lyle had faced worse things. Much worse. They could handle this. She was sure the bishop would allow her to temporarily live with Lyle, sleeping on his couch while she provided care to the widower. She would be right there to help with Lyle's needs and close to the pharmacy to make sure things were running as smoothly as possible in his absence.

When the doctor finished talking, she excused herself and left.

Lyle closed his eyes, looking worn-out. "Are you coming home to take care of me or not?"

Guilt and frustration seemed to replace Brandon's earlier concerns for his dad. "I can't. I'm sorry, Dad. I just can't. You *know* what I'm dealing with right now. We will hire someone to come in and take care of you."

"I can do it." Holly poured water from the pitcher on a nearby table into a plastic cup.

"No." Lyle's word was hard and fast. "I need you to stay focused on your routine—your work among your people, studying for the exam to get into nursing school, helping at the pharmacy full time, and preparing for the health fair. That hasn't happened yet, right?"

"It's this Saturday," she said. "That's in five days."

"Good. That means I didn't mess that up after all your hard work."

"But I can also help take care of you."

"I said no. You need to be there with your Mamm. There wouldn't really be any point in you babysitting me. You can't physically help me up the stairs to my apartment or anything else I'll need like that."

Lyle wasn't overweight, but he was quite tall and muscular for a man his age.

"Then we can hire a male nurse," Brandon said.

"Excuse me?" Lyle opened his eyes wider and stared at his son. "I don't have that sort of money. You know that."

"I . . . didn't know, actually." Brandon studied his father. "Dad," he whispered, "you're nearing retirement, and you haven't saved any money?"

"Just tell the doctor I have help, and I can be on my way in a few days. I'm sure I'll be fine."

Holly couldn't make heads or tails of what was being said. "I'm not physically strong enough to help you up the stairs, so you'll just stay by yourself?"

Brandon stared at his dad. "Who owns a pharmacy all these years and doesn't have the money to pay for care?"

Lyle looked at the ceiling. "I was hoping I would never need to tell you this. Approved cancer treatments weren't working for your mom, so we went the experimental route, but those aren't covered by insurance."

"Mom had experimental treatments? Why wasn't I told?"

"All you needed to know was that your mom was doing everything she could to get well, and she fought valiantly. I cashed my 401(k). I figured I'd be able to rebuild some savings, but the market bottomed out, and the pharmacy doesn't make the kind of money it used to."

Brandon put his hand over his face, and Holly could only imagine what all he was thinking and feeling—the frustration over his dad's secrets, the concern about the seriousness of his dad's situation, and the realization of the canyon between Lyle and him.

Brandon lowered his hand. "Okay." He pulled out his phone and tapped it a few times, clearly navigating to some piece of information. "Your insurance will cover ninety percent of your stay at a rehab facility until you're on your feet, but it won't cover a cent of hiring a private nurse, not under these circumstances. It's the way it is." He lowered his phone.

The room was silent for a bit. Holly wanted to volunteer her services again, but whatever was happening here was between a parent and his adult child.

"Look, Dad, you would tell your own patients that more than forty percent of stroke survivors suffer serious falls in the first year after their stroke. We both know you need someone there." Another heavy silence engulfed the room. "And I suppose that has to be me." Brandon's voice was softer now. Apparently Lyle's silence had won his side of the argument.

Lyle leaned back in his hospital bed, closing his eyes. Suddenly he looked very frail.

"I'll move in with you for a while and see if I can sublet my apartment, but I have to keep my Saturday job, Dad."

"I can help on Saturdays," Holly added. "But not this Saturday of course."

Lyle nodded. "The health fair."

Brandon shook his head. "We need to cancel that."

"Absolutely not." Lyle pushed a button on his bed, trying to sit up straighter. "Holly, Julie, and I began planning this more than a year ago. The work has been nonstop the last few months."

"And look where that landed you," Brandon said. "There will be time again for work. For now, I need you to focus on getting better."

"He's right." Holly folded Lyle's hand into hers. "You focus on getting better, and don't think about the health fair again. Okay?"

6

*J*oshua bent and picked up another cob of feed corn and dropped it into the harvest bag strapped to him. Boredom and frustration gnawed at him. After rushing around all morning, he had come home empty handed and had finished the chick habitats. Then the chicken supplier called and said it would be several more hours before the delivery person would arrive with the babies. He couldn't take just sitting around at home, so here he was in the neighbors' cornfield, punishing himself apparently. The neighbors were generous to allow his family to glean their harvested fields, picking up the remaining feed corn, but sometimes he wished they would be stingy.

He could not believe *that* was the pharmacy where Holly worked. Had she told him and he'd simply forgotten? He didn't think so. She never wanted to talk about work, but he'd been awed by her quirky, fun-loving confidence—an odd kind of spunk that distinguished her from the other girls. Holly seemed disinterested in attracting a guy but very interested in Ivy and her enjoying the outings. He chuckled. He'd never seen a girl so determined when it came to winning, whether on a team or playing a one-on-one game like horseshoes, badminton, or even ice-skating or racing horses.

Drop it. Just think about something else, anything other than Holly.

He ambled down the harvested rows, picking up dried ears of corn that had been left behind. The midafternoon sun warmed his back more than what was comfortable, and the smell of tilled earth hung in the air. The already-reaped rows of corn provided no shade as he worked.

The sound of tires on the gravel road roused him from the monotony. A small blue sedan pulled onto the shoulder of the field he was working and didn't stop until it was at the side of the dirt road next to his row. A pretty Amish woman with light-brown hair hopped out of the front seat, shut the door, and waved at the driver. Holly. Joshua's face warmed from more than just the afternoon sun. How had she found him, and why would she bother?

She began walking toward him, and Joshua didn't know what to do or even how to start a conversation. In his twenty-five years he'd found one woman truly interesting and had asked her out, thinking she was attracted to him too. Apparently his request was so offensive that she felt it necessary to stop coming to all singles functions. Ignoring her, he drew a breath and picked up two more cobs. His mother would be so proud of his manners.

"Hallo." Her pleasant voice indicated she was just a few feet away. He glanced up and saw that she had strapped on one of the harvest bags he'd left on the end of the row. She picked up a cob of corn.

"Hi." He stopped the work and stood up. How could he make his earlier rudeness right? "I'm, uh, sorry for this morning. Is he okay?"

"Ya." She scooped up several more cobs. "Well, okay enough for now. It'll take some time for him to recover, but he seems to be out of danger."

"Gut." What could he say that wouldn't make him look worse in her eyes? "Why'd you come find me?" He'd tried to voice the question in a gentle way, but it still sounded rude.

"I told you I'd bring the medicine."

"Ya, and I appreciate it, but why are you *here*?" He gestured at the rows of harvested corn.

"You were stressed this morning, worried about your Mamm. I was on my way to the address on the prescription and saw you in the field." She stopped, reached a hand into her hidden apron pocket, and pulled out a white paper bag. "This is insulin, so I knew she probably needed it today. Since it requires at least a room-temperature environment, I could take it by your house if you're going to be in the field for a while. My driver will be back within ten minutes. He is just giving me a bit of time while he looks for a gas station or convenience store to buy a soda. And just as general info, insulin should be kept in the fridge during the summertime for those who don't have air conditioning, and it should never be stored somewhere that's above eighty degrees. But in this October weather, it's fine staying with you for the next hour as long as it's not in the direct sun."

"Good to know, but it's okay. I'll take it. I'm about picked out and was planning to head back home soon."

"Well, good then." She handed the bag to him.

He folded it and tucked it into his pants pocket. "Denki."

She smiled, and of all the smiles Joshua had seen, hers was the best. Was she seeing someone? He couldn't ask, but he did wonder why they'd had six months of fun—camaraderie even—and yet one simple request for a date had caused her to run away and hide. On the other hand, if he wanted her to leave right now, he knew how to get rid of her—and fast.

But he wouldn't do that. With all she'd been through today, she'd remembered his Mamm. Maybe the many good things he'd heard about Greene's Pharmacy since his Mamm landed in the hospital Saturday were true. "My Mamm . . . she's not been herself lately. I don't know how much is physical and how much is emotional."

Holly started walking again, picking up corn as she went. "It's hard when someone we care about is sick."

"Seems like it." He strolled beside her, picking up corn too. "I'm sorry about this morning." He'd said that once already, but he'd sounded half-hearted, and she hadn't acknowledged hearing it.

She turned to face him and gave another smile. "Please don't give that another thought. If you have any questions about the medicine, Adrienne or Harris, our other pharmacists, will be able to answer them. I have a cell, and we can get them answered now if you want." She went back to walking down the row of corn.

"Why are you being so nice?" He motioned toward the harvesting bag she was carrying.

She put more corn in her bag. "Because I've been where you are—worried about a parent. And because it's very hard to offend me about work stuff. Each person who walks through our door could be having the worst day of his or her life due to health issues—theirs or a family member's. We often see people at their worst emotionally and physically, and it's our job to give them the tools they need to make things better."

"That's really an amazing outlook to have."

She plunked more corn into the harvest bag. "I will say, though, that usually the type of rudeness you displayed is reserved for the chronically ill. Are you ill, Josh?" Her lips curled into a wry smile.

He grinned at her teasing. She had to have a dozen guys vying for her attention, and he was bound to be the only one who'd been rude to her. Again, his Mamm would be so proud.

She jiggled the bulging harvest bag and nodded toward the wagon, clearly ready to empty the bag of its contents. "Is this for your chickens?"

"No. I needed to glean this field sooner or later, and since a shipment of chicks I was expecting earlier today was delayed in transit, now was as good a time as any. But baby chickens need a special corn, not this stuff, and they need it milled with a specific formula for their health, and the grown chickens don't eat corn. They forage on their own for grubs, worms, and weeds. But we have other animals on the farm that need feed corn—a really grumpy mule we use to keep foxes away from the chickens, a dairy cow we milk for personal use, and goats that only eat feed in the winter when there isn't enough grass."

"You're not the grumpy mule that guards the henhouse, are you?"

He laughed. "You know, now that you mention it, I think sometimes I am."

She chuckled. "The number for the pharmacy is on the instruction insert and the box holding the vial of insulin. Just call if you or your Mamm ends up having any questions."

"I believe we are set. She was in the hospital over the weekend. That's when she got the diagnosis. She came home with a small supply of insulin to get her through until this evening, and the doctors were clear in their instructions on how to use it." Wait, why was he trying to end the conversation? "But actually . . . I am curious about something. I don't think I've ever met an Amish woman who works in health care. I didn't realize that about you when we got to know each other."

"What?" She put her hands on her hips. "I told you I worked at a small pharmacy."

"Ya. And I have two sisters who used to work at Home Depot before they got married, and neither of them knew anything about home repair or the products. They knew how to operate the register and the scanner that rang up the sales. That's it." He shook a corncob at her. "But that's not you. When I saw the brass key to the store in your hand, I got a feeling that place was a part of you. And the way you waltzed inside, welcoming me, it seemed clear that you're a part of Greene's Pharmacy in a way that goes much deeper than working the register."

She lifted her hand to her brows, blocking the sun from her eyes while studying him. "That's strangely observant."

"Ya, anytime the word *strange* is used, it somehow ends up being connected to me."

She gave a short laugh. "That's not necessarily a bad thing."

So maybe this strange set of circumstances would give him a second chance with her. They paused behind the wagon, and when she removed the bag, Joshua took it from her and emptied the corn into the wagon. "Just how connected are you to Greene's Pharmacy?"

"Very. I know it's unusual for any Amish to be this coupled with health care, but I have the full support of my bishop. I started working for Lyle after my Daed died when I was fourteen. I joined the church at seventeen, and my bishop allowed me to get my GED and to continue to work full time. Once I had my GED, I qualified to take a state board exam to be a pharmacy technician. That was no easy feat. Now I'm studying for the entrance exam into nursing school. If . . . *When* I get in, I'll take classes at the pace of a snail, like one class a semester, until I'm an LPN."

"Wait . . ." He blinked a few times. "You have your GED, and you're planning to go to college?"

"Ya, sorry. Maybe I should've told you that last year, but the bishop asked that I keep it to myself as much as possible. The ministers and I are trying not to stir up trouble, because if anyone complains to the bishop, and especially if a group comes to him, he'll probably have to ask me to quit. But I need that license. See, if you or anyone has a question about a medicine I deliver, I can't legally answer, even if every word I said was correct or if I read the answer off the insert that came with your medicine."

"That's sort of crazy."

"I think so too, but it's the law, and they probably have good reasons for it. Once I'm an LPN, I can give answers. Then I'll have to call a pharmacist only when I don't know something."

"I asked a friend about you when you came to the first gathering, so I knew you'd joined the church as a teen." Joshua had yet to join. He loved music, specifically the guitar. He'd been taking lessons for years, and all that had to end when he joined. "But I figured you'd had a beau and intended to marry and that things hadn't worked out."

"What? No. Why does everyone have to assume that the only thing single women are interested in is marriage?"

"Because ninety-eight percent of the time it's true for Amish girls, but I didn't mean to offend you."

"I doubt you'd understand what family life entails for a woman. It's not just frowned on if we wish to continue working after marriage. It's forbidden, at the very least for the first year. By then a baby has arrived or will soon, and the woman's place is to stay home. My work is too important. Speaking of that, we are actually having a health fair specifically for the Amish this Saturday in Raysburg Field behind the Martel Clinic. You remember, that's where your Mamm saw Doc Jules. You'd like the clinic's owner, Doc Martel, too."

He was beginning to get a fresh perspective on why she might have turned him down and disappeared. In truth he wasn't quite sure how he felt about such strong opinions coming from a woman. Maybe she'd done them both a favor by refusing even one date.

"Ya, I heard a little something about that."

The small blue car that had dropped her off earlier was slowly approaching them.

Holly waved him forward. "You should come, Josh, and bring your Mamm. There will be so much helpful information, answers that could otherwise take years to piece together, and you'll receive handouts to take home. Julie—Doc Jules—will explain everything in detail, and then she'll open the floor for questions. People will ask questions you might not think to ask, and, voilà, you'll have answers before you knew you needed them."

"You know, it can't hurt anything to go."

"Can't hurt a thing. Might even be useful." She grinned. "Free, useful info is hard to beat."

The word *free* jogged a thought. "What about payment for the insulin? I know money talks, but we're surrounded by corncobs, and they're pretty quiet, being all ears and no lips."

She laughed. "Observant and witty." She dusted off her dress. "I can start a tab for you and your family at the pharmacy. Come by at your convenience to pay it."

He smiled. "Denki, Holly."

How did one of the most boring activities in the world suddenly turn into the brightest spot of his day? Same way the gatherings suddenly became fun. Holly was involved. But what did it say about him that the only girl he connected with wasn't interested in following the traditional path?

7

*F*amiliar aromas and noises from Brandon's childhood caused dozens of memories to wallop him as he walked through the pharmacy with his dad beside him. Well, two things were new. The feel of his dad's knobby elbow in the palm of Brandon's hand as he guided his aging dad toward the steps that led to his apartment and the sound of his dad's cane thudding against the floor. It'd only been three days since his dad's stroke, but in many ways it felt as if weeks had passed. Brandon hadn't wasted any time. He'd subleased his bedroom in the apartment, moved his stuff out to make room for the new guy, and spent restless hours studying for the upcoming exam while at his dad's bedside in the hospital.

Now they methodically made their way toward their destination, and Brandon figured this was what life would look like for a while—moving like a turtle. But rather than Dad continuing toward the stairs, he eased toward the pharmacy counter.

"Dad, come on." Brandon tugged gently, biting his tongue to keep from speaking the frustrations in his head. He silently prayed for patience. "Upstairs. You can't work right now." His dad had *no clue* what kind of sacrifice Brandon was making by moving back to his hometown, even temporarily.

His dad gave a dismissive wave and escaped Brandon's guiding hand.

He continued toward the prescription work area instead of their intended destination: the side door to the apartment upstairs.

"Really? You are really going to step behind that counter?" Brandon shook his head.

"Holly! Adrienne!" his dad called, sounding as if he were greeting his employees on a normal day.

Though Brandon was staring at his dad's retreating back, he was sure that a big grin was plastered across Dad's face, albeit lopsided from the stroke. A familiar annoyance rose in Brandon's chest. His dad never failed to treat his employees as if they were family, even at the expense of his actual family.

Adrienne was blank faced and blinked several times before smiling. "Lyle? What on earth are you doing behind this counter? Your son told me you are supposed to be in bed."

Adrienne's white pharmacist coat needed an iron, her usually well-kept red hair was in disarray, and she had dark circles under her eyes. She had twins who were almost two, and as a relief pharmacist, she worked only on Thursdays and Saturdays and sometimes on the very rare occasion Lyle needed to take a sick day. But she was here, filling in for his dad and working every other shift since Lyle's stroke. But neither Adrienne nor Harris could work here full time. Brandon had to get a full-time temporary pharmacist-in-charge as soon as possible. He'd talked to someone about that yesterday. Brandon thought his dad would approve of his choice, but right now the most important thing was to get his dad settled upstairs and resting.

"Lyle . . ." Holly put a hand on her hip. "Put your lab coat back on its peg and go upstairs. You need rest. We've got this under control."

"What's going on? How behind are we?" Dad ignored her instructions.

"You don't wanna know." Adrienne laughed in a short, high-pitched chuckle.

"Come 'ere, Son." Lyle inched his way forward, leaning on his cane. "Let's spend a few minutes and help them out."

"Dad." Brandon clenched his teeth. "We are literally walking in from a three-day hospital stay. You are in no condition to check *any* scripts right now."

"I'm not a moron, Bran. I'm not going to verify any scripts. I'm just going to help our hardworking ladies catch up. It's about time for the afternoon rush."

"We already have four people in the store waiting on prescriptions we said would be done thirty minutes ago," Adrienne added.

Not helpful, Brandon wanted to tell her. It was clear there was no talking his dad out of this.

"Fine." Brandon yanked a spare white pharmacist coat off the peg. "We'll help for ten minutes. Then you and I are going upstairs and getting you settled in."

Twenty-five minutes in, Brandon was kicking himself for not considering the rule of pharmacy busyness: every problem you solve often creates several others. Holly was typing and furiously scanning data entry, trying to get to the bottom of the stack of scripts in the queue. His dad was pulling medications from the shelf and arranging the baskets in order. Adrienne was counting pills and double-checking Holly's typing against the scanned prescription copies and also verifying they had the right medication and the possible drug interactions. Brandon found himself working the register and manning the phone, answering questions, taking phoned-in prescriptions from doctors, and ringing up the finished prescriptions. It was helpful that he could legally dispense information as a licensed pharmacy graduate intern. Between ringing up customers at the register, he answered the phone. With the pharmacy this busy, why wasn't his dad making any money?

"Holly,"—Dad paused from putting bottles of meds into a basket—"have you taken a break at all today?"

Brandon doubted it. Who could step away with this kind of busyness? He had the handset to the push-button phone cradled between his shoulder and ear, on hold with a doctor's office. He'd been stuck like this for several minutes. He could see the light on the pharmacy phone flashing with two more calls waiting. He glanced up at Holly. Her hands were shaking as she typed.

"Well, I . . ." Holly trailed off, eyes still on the computer screen.

"I think that's Holly-ese for *no.*" Lyle chuckled. "Why don't you take five? Go sit down. Maybe get some water and a protein bar from the drawer in the break room while Brandon and I are here."

Brandon shifted the phone against his shoulder, waiting for the nurse to come on the line. "This coming from you? You shouldn't be here working, period, and you agreed you would go upstairs after ten minutes of helping." But his dad was right. Holly needed to take a break. Not doing so broke all sorts of labor regulations, and it made her more susceptible to making mistakes. The last thing this pharmacy needed was the State Board of Pharmacy on their backs or a tech making a mistake that an exhausted pharmacist wouldn't catch. "Yeah, Holly, he's right. You need to take a break. After I get finished with this call, I'll work on data entry in between patients."

Holly nodded and headed to the break room.

"Dad, when I wrap up this phone call, you are going upstairs."

"I'm needed here, Brandon. I'm feeling good."

"But you agreed to . . ."

His dad didn't seem to notice Brandon was talking to him. His aging father hummed to himself, as if he was pleased with his successful coup to avoid bed rest.

Brandon watched his dad look up and down a shelf for a med. The pharmacy had the same organizational setup now as it had since its opening, so there was no way it should take him this long to find a common drug. "Look, you're either going upstairs or back to the hospital. Your choice."

"May I remind you that I'm the parent and I own this building? I'm not old enough *yet* for you to take over my affairs."

"I didn't give up my own life, study time, and actual paid hours to stand beside you in this pharmacy while you have another stroke."

Dad finally found the medicine he was looking for and placed it in the basket he was holding. "They need help."

Then hire more help! This small pharmacy felt busier than his Saturdays as an intern at BB Drugs in Philadelphia. There should be enough profits on the weekends to support hiring help.

Brandon watched his dad from the corner of his eye, wishing he could stop this chaos and just get him up the stairs and into bed. Finally he heard the click of the doctor's office line reconnecting.

"Dr. Rodger's office." A clipped female voice answered. Had she forgotten that she left him on hold?

"Yes, this is Brandon over at Greene's Pharmacy. We're filling insulin for one of your patients, and the script says 'use as directed.'"

"Yes . . ."

"With those instructions it's not legal to bill an insurance company. We need specific instructions or a maximum number of units to use per day." He gave her the patient's name and birthday.

She scoffed. "Well, the patient's been on that same med for years and knows how to use it."

"I understand that, but the insurance company has protocols. Legally, we can't fill the script as it's currently written. I'm sure you understand—"

"I'll call you later after I speak with the doctor." *Click*. Brandon bet it would be a few hours before they heard back from the office—if they heard at all—and the patient surely would end up frustrated with the pharmacy.

Brandon had just hung up the phone when it rang again. He jerked it from its cradle, hoping to sound professional. "Greene's Pharmacy. This is Brandon. How may I help you?"

"I heard Doc Lyle had some sort of serious illness. I wanted to check on him."

Brandon pulled air into his lungs and counted to three. "Lyle is doing well. He'll be out for a few weeks recuperating, but the pharmacy will keep its regular hours with a pharmacist here to serve all customers as needed."

"So what about the health fair that's supposed to be held this Saturday? Is that still taking place?"

His dad staggered, and the prescription basket in his hand with its bottle and papers went flying. *Dad!* Brandon dropped the phone and lunged forward, reaching for his dad. Somehow he managed to grab his dad by the chest and just barely keep him from banging his head against the pharmacy counter. He guided his dad's body upright, returned his cane to him, and stared at his face. It didn't appear to be another stroke. Just a stumble. A stumble that could have landed Dad back in the hospital with another concussion.

"This is enough." Brandon barely kept his voice from yelling. "We are going upstairs *now*."

Adrienne stared wide eyed at Brandon as he raised his voice to his father. The eyes of the few nearby customers were on him. Somehow the tables had turned, and he sounded like the parent scolding a child who had gotten himself into danger.

"My foot must have caught on the shelf corner," his father mumbled, his voice shaking.

The phone's handset was bobbing up and down, its black coil cord dangling from the pharmacy counter.

"Hallo? Hallo? Anyone there?"

Adrienne answered it. "Hello. This is Adrienne. May I help you?"

The voice on the other end came through faintly. "No. I need to talk to that Brandon guy I was talking to. No one else."

Brandon steadied his dad, supporting him firmly under his forearm as he guided him toward the exit gate of the pharmacy.

"Brandon, the man on the phone insists on speaking to you."

He took the handset. "This is Brandon Greene."

"Ya, we were talking about the health fair, and something happened. You're Lyle's boy, right? So what's the plan about the health fair?"

"I don't have a good answer for you, but as far as I'm concerned, it should be canceled. My dad just had a stroke, and I need to focus on him, not on anything else." He dropped the receiver into its cradle, hoping the man would get a clue and stop calling with questions that had nothing to do with running the pharmacy.

At the pace of that proverbial turtle, Brandon helped his dad up the stairs.

"I'm needed in the pharmacy."

"No, you need to rest and recuperate. I talked with Todd Thompson yesterday."

"Todd?" His dad didn't sound impressed, but maybe he was just out of breath.

Brandon held firmly to his dad's elbow as they continued up the stairs. "Yeah, I thought you'd like the idea of your former employee filling in for you. It's been ten years since he quit, but he knows the store and probably still knows a lot of the customers."

"That's true, but . . ." Dad breathed deeply as they finally got to the landing.

Garbage bags filled with Brandon's stuff from his room in the apartment were pushed up against the walls of the oversized landing. He had been fortunate to find a student who wanted to sublease the room. Brandon was probably charging the young man too little, as the money didn't quite cover his portion of the rent that he was still responsible for. But he had to fill the spot as soon as possible, and he'd need the room back, hopefully next month. There was no point in unpacking.

"Dad, Todd has taken off time from his regular job with BB Drugs to help out. I can't believe his company agreed to let Harris do this for the last five years, and now they're letting Todd do the same. But since they're a huge company, I guess they have plenty of floater pharmacists, so they can have a pretty lenient policy." Brandon unlocked the apartment door and opened it. "I know you and Todd had a disagreement ten years ago, but he wants to lend a hand during this time, and Greene's Pharmacy can't afford to look a gift horse in the mouth."

While his dad sat in his recliner, catching his breath, Brandon slunk into the kitchen. He opened the fridge, hoping there was something edible inside. Annoyance pounded, much like his head. But thankfully there was a foil-covered dish with a note on top from Holly's mom.

"Hey." Dad's voice was quiet.

Brandon turned. "You need something?"

His dad looked so different from the man of Brandon's childhood. Dad held firmly to the cane in his hand as he leaned against the door-frame for support. His chest was still heaving, probably from the meds to regulate his heart. "No . . ." Dad shook his head. "Well, yeah. I guess." He had something on his mind.

"There's no time for shyness. Just spit it out. What do you need me to do?"

"Nothing. I just . . . well . . . Thanks for dropping everything to be here for me. And thanks for getting Todd to help out. I don't mean to sound ungrateful. You're doing more than I deserve, and—"

"Don't." Brandon lifted his hand. As frustrated as he was with having to live here for now and reduce his work hours at his dream company, he was acutely aware of how blessed he was to still have his father, mind mostly intact, after a stroke. But they didn't have to exchange a lot of emotional stuff that his dad wouldn't have said if he hadn't come so close to dying. "I'm glad you're okay, and we'll get through this, but you are going to follow the doctor's orders to a T and focus on recovering. I'll handle everything else. Okay?"

8

*S*unrays peeped over the horizon, illuminating hills that were nearing their peak autumn color, as Holly drove toward town. She kept blinking in an effort to ease the dryness and grittiness in her eyes. Her lack of sleep aside, today was perfect, everything she'd spent years praying for—excellent health-care providers at booths, community support, and a clear Indian summer October day.

"How're ya holding up?" Ivy leaned back and stretched as far as her arms could go above her head in the buggy. "I could have helped you more last night on the preparations. You didn't have to order me to bed."

"I'm great, and that's what big sisters do—order you young uns around." She stifled a yawn. "Besides, I need your mind functioning at full capacity if you are going to oversee and direct our setup."

Although Holly had tied the last bow on the tulle-encased giveaways around three this morning, she felt rejuvenated by the anticipation of this event she had worked on tirelessly for months. It was all coming together. Next time it wouldn't take more than a year to pull together a solid health fair. She'd made good connections, learned a lot, and taken impeccable notes.

Dew on the grass sparkled as she pulled into Raysburg Field. This simple field was usually empty except to shelter a few horses for Amish customers and workers in the downtown area. But in just a short time, she and the other volunteers would transform it into the most amazing health fair the town had ever seen.

"Arriving on majestic Raysburg Field"—Ivy spread her arms open wide—"our team's star player: Holly! Will she bring it home or choke in the ninth inning due to staying up all night?" Ivy directed her best baseball-announcer voice into her hand "microphone" as Holly slowed Stevie to a stop in front of the hitching post.

Holly pursed her lips together and glared at her sister, who met her annoyance with a giant grin. "Oh hush, you. I'm not the star player. Those would be the actual professionals who volunteered to be here. Or the brave Amish who will come to get a checkup for the first time." She shoved a clipboard into her sister's hands. "If I were you, I'd keep to myself that familiarity with what professional baseball announcers sound like before the ministers realize you do more than just clean when you're in Englisch homes." Holly shooed her away. "Now take your pestering and put it to good use."

Ivy laughed and pretended to swat her older sister with the clipboard. She hopped out of the buggy. Holly had full faith in her little sister to do a great job directing all the volunteers in the setup. Ivy had a knack for getting people to work together but in such a gentle, lighthearted way that they wouldn't realize how hard they were working.

Holly jumped down, tethered Stevie to the hitching post, and surveyed the green space. It seemed she had timed her arrival perfectly with the rental company who was putting up the tents. There was no time to stand around. The to-do list in her sweater pocket was burning a hole in the fabric. Could she get her portion of the work done and be ready in four hours? Unlike Ivy, who would greet all the workers and volunteers and help them get set up, Holly would hide out in the largest event tent to do all her tasks.

She pushed her sweater sleeves up past her elbows, stacked two boxes together, and carried them to a table she would use for giveaways.

The time went by quickly as she put up partitions to provide privacy for the individual well checks. She then put the right equipment in each cubicle according to the marked boxes Julie had given her.

Holly wiped sweat off her forehead and took stock of all she'd done. *Oh, signs.* She pulled several from a box and hung the appropriate ones on each partitioned section of the tent. This was the largest tent she'd rented, and it now looked perfect for giving people a reasonable amount of privacy. She couldn't help but grin. Today numerous Amish people who'd ignored their health for years, perhaps for decades, would get a good checkup and consultation.

The flap on the tent door opened. "Excuse me, Miss Zook?" A man in an EMT uniform entered. "The young woman with a clipboard told me to come find you." He gestured out the tent door. "The fire truck is here, and we were wondering where we need to pull in."

"Here, already?" What time was it? She reached for her cell, but it wasn't in her pocket. It dawned on her that she hadn't seen it since arriving. Her best guess was that in her hurry to get out the door with all the stuff in tow, she hadn't grabbed her phone.

The man looked at his watch. "It's quarter of ten. Did I get the time mixed up?"

"Oh no. I just lost track of time." She imagined the joy of little boys and girls when they got to climb on the massive red fire engine. Excitement pumped through her, making her smile. "Come on. I'll show you." Holly stepped out of the tent.

The midmorning sun was bright, and she once again noted how perfect the weather was for a health fair. But where were the Amish? It dawned on her how quiet things were as she'd set up inside her tent. There should've been lots of voices as background noise while she worked for the last twenty or so minutes.

The different medical vendors were ready to go under large white event tents that had bold print signs advertising their services. In the center of the field, the tables of healthy fruits and vegetables donated from the locally owned grocery store down the road stood in full bounty and made her mouth water. In her nervousness about getting everything done on time this morning, she had forgotten to eat breakfast. As she led the EMT toward the place the truck would park, she walked by teens from the nearby *Englischer* high school who had set up a few health-themed science fair exhibits. They were standing around and giggling among themselves.

She smiled broadly. "Good morning."

She received an out-of-sync chorus of hellos.

"The truck should go right over here." She gestured to a roped-off area on the field that had a sign marked EMT. The EMT removed the flagging that stretched from one stake to another and signaled to the driver, who waved at them and pulled the truck into the space.

Holly searched the field, looking for groups of Amish or rigs. Where was everyone? She pointed. "You can set up your twelve-lead EKG screening in this tent. You have the sign, correct?"

"Yes ma'am."

"Are you sure of the time?" Judging by the sun's position, the man had told her correctly. But if that was right, why weren't more Amish people here?

He pulled out a phone and looked at the time. "My watch is right. It's now five till ten."

Holly's heart turned a flip. Something was wrong. Five minutes before time to start and almost no one was here? "I thought we'd have more people by now."

The EMT shrugged. "I was thinking the same thing."

She thanked him and left. Maybe there was a large gathering on the other side of the tents that were looming in front of her. She hurried across the grounds.

Almost no one except volunteers and vendors. What was going on?

She took a deep breath, trying to quell the rising panic that threatened to knock her feet out from under her. She had counted ten Amish so far. *Ten.* They were expecting nearly two hundred. Had the wrong information about the starting time gone out to people? That didn't seem possible. She'd made the flyers herself and triple-checked everything.

She hurried through the center of the grassy field, nodding and smiling at the medical vendors. She hoped her smile seemed genuine and hid the anxiety eating at her. Everything and everyone was ready and waiting for her people.

At last she reached Julie's station. A few Englischers were there, probably people who'd been shopping in the area and were drawn to the field by the tents, bringing Holly's visitor count to around twenty-five.

"Hey there, Holly Noelle." Julie smiled as if nothing were out of the ordinary. "You look like you need to sit down for a spell." Julie pulled out a plastic folding chair.

Holly shook her head. "What happened, Jules?" Tears brimmed, threatening to spill over. "Where are all my people?"

Julie shrugged. "Sometimes these things happen, but I don't know why our turnout is this bad. Are you sure your bishop was as supportive as you thought? Perhaps there was some dissention you were unaware of." Julie separated different papers with information on diabetes into stacks.

"Surely not!"

"Well, all we can do is make the best of it, right? Try to spread the word that my first fifteen-minute diabetes class will begin in a few minutes in case the visitors didn't see the posters."

Holly's cheeks burned with embarrassment. Although Julie was being so kind, Holly was quite aware of how valuable her time was as a medical professional, as was the time of all the people who had volunteered. Holly had been the one to push for this fair, to contact all the vendors, to ask that people donate their time and resources. This fair represented more than a year's worth of work for her.

Tears filled her eyes again. Where could she go to get a minute alone? She walked around to the opposite side of Julie's tent, away from the eyes of the volunteers and the very small crowd that had come, and took a deep breath. How could today be such a failure?

Her legs shook, and she sat down in the dew-covered grass, not caring if her dress got wet. Hidden away from the meager number of visitors, she drew her knees to her chest and covered her face with her arms. She finally allowed the tears to fall, darkening the fabric of her half apron and plum-colored dress.

Today was supposed to quietly honor her Daed's life, to acknowledge the huge hole he'd left while finding ways to prevent others from experiencing a similar unnecessary loss. But now the funds for advertising, renting tents, and providing medical supplies were gone. So much effort for nothing. How could she ask the health-care professionals and vendors to come to another fair after this fiasco?

The disaster of this health fair, Lyle's stroke, and the looming concerns about Greene's ability to stay open long term—it was all too much.

How could she possibly fix it all?

9

*J*oshua looked out the window of the car as the driver took him by Raysburg Field, going toward the entry to the parking lot. The scene on the field made little sense. If his Mamm was right that the health fair had been called off, why was he seeing a fire truck, EMTs, vendors of all types, and a huge white tent with the sign Free Health Screening?

And yet almost no one was here.

He'd come to attend the diabetes class—if his Mamm was wrong and the event was still taking place. If it wasn't, he'd go to Greene's and speak to whoever was working today about Mamm's next steps in managing her diabetes. Either way he would learn more about his Mamm's diagnosis, and perhaps he would have an opportunity to talk to a particularly attractive and fascinating pharmacy tech. Her rejection should have settled the matter, and her view that her work was more important than any relationship should have confirmed the matter. Yet here he was, hoping for a good reason to strike up another conversation with her.

What was it about her anyway?

He wasn't sure, but in the five days since they'd talked, he had realized he liked her strong opinions. And was it so very wrong for a woman to keep working outside the home after marriage?

The driver pulled into a parking space in front of the sidewalk and put the car in Park. "I'd heard about this fair last week and was hopeful I could get a free health screening, but then your mother said it was canceled. By the look of it, maybe I can get that screening today after all."

"Ya, maybe so."

They got out of the car and walked toward the tents. His driver went to the tent with the free-screening sign in front of it. Joshua spotted the doc lady his Mamm had seen while in the hospital. Well, she wasn't a real doctor. She was some kind of really educated nurse, but the Amish called her Doc Jules. She was setting up an easel on the lawn under a small canopy. He strode that way. She tried to get a large whiteboard onto the tripod, but she dropped it, sending several markers flying through the air.

"Need a hand?" he asked.

Without looking up she pushed her straight, shoulder-length hair from her face. "Please."

He picked up the oversize dry-erase board and put it on the easel. She grabbed the markers off the ground. "Thank you. It isn't that heavy, but it slid right out of my hands anyway." She put the markers back in the tray and then turned to him. "Oh, uh, Joshua Smucker, right?" Her forehead crinkled as if she was unsure.

"That's right. I'm surprised you remembered."

"I was hoping someone from your family would come today so we could talk more about your mom's new diagnosis."

"Ya, Holly told me it was important."

"It is." Doc Jules gestured to a group of chairs gathered under the canopy. "Take a seat. My first class is about to start."

Joshua sat down. Only one other person was waiting for the class.

Doc Jules stepped in front of the chairs and smiled. "Good morning! You know the best thing about a small group? We can go really deep into any questions you have."

Fifteen minutes later he'd reviewed the proper technique for taking blood sugar and the guidelines for when it should be taken. He'd learned more details about the symptoms of low and high blood sugar and the signs that would indicate Mamm needed to go to the hospital. Doc Jules even handed out a diabetic-friendly recipe packet. The class dispersed, and Joshua stood.

He scanned the field. He figured he'd spot Holly walking around, checking on things or helping here and there. No luck. He turned back to Doc Jules. "Thanks again for the info. Have you seen Holly?"

Doc Jules was erasing the whiteboard. She paused and looked across the field. "Not since the class began. But last I saw her, she was going around the side of that tent."

Given Holly's refusal to go out with him, it made a lot more sense for him not to look for her. But apparently he would defy logic and common sense. Only God knew why. "Thanks." He started to walk off.

Doc Jules set the dry eraser next to the markers. "Did you need something or have any questions?"

"No, thank you." He glanced back at the field with its bountiful tents and sparse people. "But my guess is this is a rough day for Holly." Was the rumor of the fair being canceled why he was so bent on coming today? An intuition that Holly would need a friend? That would at least make more sense than chasing after her just because he was attracted to her.

Doc Jules glanced at the wide-open spaces between the tents and vendors. "You're right." She smiled. "Go." One side of her mouth curved upward.

"Sure thing." He walked the length of the huge tent, and when he rounded the corner, he saw Holly sitting on the ground, studying something in the distance. He wasn't sure whether to speak or leave her alone. "Holly . . ."

She turned. When their eyes met, she looked away.

He didn't need her to tell him that he wasn't who she wanted to see right now. "Is there someone I can get for you?"

She wiped her eyes with her apron and sat up straighter. Was she trying to hide that she'd been crying? "No. I'm . . . fine." Her voice broke, and he was pretty sure she could use a friend.

He sat down in the wet grass next to her.

She swiped her fingers across her cheeks. "You're going to get dew and grass all over you."

"Ya and maybe worse since this field is normally used for horses. Still don't care." He leaned in. "You okay?"

"Ya, of course." She shrugged.

Should he pretend to believe her? He could hear a few people walking and talking on the other side of the tent, but it was nowhere near the boisterous sounds of the crowd she'd said would be here. Why had the pharmacist said that the fair was canceled? Should he just ask her, or would that make it worse?

What am I supposed to say? His thought was really more a prayer, and he immediately knew the answer—the truth, as fully as he knew it, with no assumptions added.

He cleared his throat. "I'm sorry you're hurt."

"Denki." She wiped her cheek again. "I'm disappointed more than anything." She stared at a spot near the horizon. "That's the back road where traffic converges to get here. I keep sitting here, half expecting a line of buggies to fill the emptiness. Is something else going on in the Amish community today? Have I been so busy I didn't realize there's a community work frolic or mission outreach today? People need to be here, for their sakes. The information they'd get today would improve the quality of health for entire families and save lives. Do you know how many people are walking around with undetected issues like high blood pressure, heart disease, or even cancers?"

Now wasn't the time to tell her that Brandon had canceled the fair. She needed to talk, and maybe, just maybe, she needed to know his thoughts. Joshua stretched out his legs. "Ya, I hear you, but sometimes health situations are out of our control, no matter how much we wish we could fix them. Like my Mamm developing bad sugars. Like your boss. He's as educated on these things as they come, but he had a stroke."

Holly sniffed. "You can't be serious, Josh. Are you saying that because some people have a health crisis—like Lyle and his stroke—we should give up and accept whatever comes to all of us, as if other issues aren't preventable? That's like saying because some people will develop certain illnesses no matter what they do, none of us should put any effort into being healthy." She stared at him, and he didn't see the same girl who'd come to the singles events. That Holly was warm and funny and loved good, competitive games of volleyball, badminton, and horseshoes. She laughed and teased. This girl was driven, haunted by desires he couldn't understand.

"People get sick, Holly. Some get better. Some don't. It's been that way for thousands and thousands of years."

"But the key is using knowledge to bring some sort of control to as many health issues as possible."

"But that's just it. Even when we do everything right within our power, life can hit us upside the head with a compost bucket. It gets messy." He feigned wiping an imagined mess of compost off his face and arms. Did she have any idea what he was mimicking?

A smile tugged at her lips. "I take it you know this from experience?"

"Youngest of thirteen. You bet I do."

"I'm the oldest of only three." Holly plucked a few blades of grass from the ground. "My parents wanted more but never got a chance because they had fertility issues, and the church frowns on getting help. Then my Daed died young. It started as strep. If he'd just taken his medicine, it wouldn't have developed into sepsis. I wish every day he'd understood the importance of going to the doctor in time, but he was steeped in believing that all he needed to do was put the situation in God's hands. Understanding an illness can be the difference between life and death, between getting better or not."

Joshua couldn't think of anything to say for several moments. But he believed he understood her—or at least more of her than before. "You want to make sure that other Amish families don't lose a loved one due to something preventable," he whispered.

"Exactly. And I've seen that it's possible. I can't tell you how badly I wish I'd understood its importance before losing Daed. But now I get the unbelievable blessing of making a difference. One time I convinced a young Amish mother to get a health screening. When she followed my advice, Julie found a suspicious mole and referred her to a dermatologist. I went with her to the appointment. The dermatologist removed the spot, tested it, and it came back as melanoma. That's a cancer that's often deadly if it progresses past the skin, but thanks to a minor surgery and some medicine Lyle filled at Greene's, she's alive. An entire family exists because she took good advice and made her health a priority."

"That's remarkable, but—"

"She was one person. One life. What kind of difference could be made if everyone understood? I mean really understood the power that's in their hands. Every goal I've tried to achieve in the past ten years has been focused on bringing knowledge to our people. Then no one showed up today. I thought I'd made some real headway in bringing together modern medicine and the Old Ways."

Clearly a fire burned inside her about this, yet how realistic were her goals? "But even the Englisch, with all their education and available information, can't prevent most illnesses. Just like what happened to your boss. It's why a lot of people like me and my parents have always had the mind-set to leave our health in God's hands."

She played with the blades of grass as if pondering what she would share and what she would hold back. "Is that how you feel about your chickens? My guess is you follow every piece of information you can get your hands on to keep them healthy. You stay proactive, as Lyle calls it. And after your best efforts to keep them well, if a few show symptoms of illness, you do everything in your power to keep it from spreading, and you try to get the sick ones well."

"Well, ya, of course I tend to them. The chickens are my family's livelihood, and it's my God-given responsibility to tend to them. But mankind is in God's hands."

The preachers and his family always said the beginning and ending of people's days were in God's hands, and he'd always accepted that as the way things should be. Was he wrong, or was she?

She plucked several blades of grass by the roots. "You've just described most Amish. We care for God's earth and the creatures we make a living with, but we ignore *our* needs."

His chest suddenly felt odd, as if floodwater was lifting his house off its foundation. "I see . . . I think." He rubbed his forehead, boggled at the confusion she'd stirred.

"Josh, that's just the tip of the iceberg when it comes to understanding the issues facing the Amish."

"Like?"

She shook her head. "I've said plenty."

"Why?" He really wanted to hear more. Maybe he'd find flaws in what she was saying. Maybe he wouldn't. But he wasn't ready for this conversation to end.

"Because anything else will sound as if I'm attacking you and your beliefs."

"I can deal with it, and I'd really like to know."

She fidgeted with the blades of grass, saying nothing.

"Kumm on, Holly."

She nodded. "See, I know that once you realized your Mamm needed a doctor and medicine, you've done your best, but did you know her diabetes might have been preventable?"

"What?" His brows knit. "Nee. She was healthy except for the natural issues that come with getting older. She's been active all her life and isn't overweight."

"I would guess she only saw a doctor when sick."

"Well, ya. Sure. That saves time and money."

"Diabetes often starts with elevated sugar in the blood that can easily be detected by simple tests during annual checkups. What is now full-blown diabetes might have started a decade ago or more, and her doctor would've caught the signs early and recommended a lot of things to prevent the situation from getting worse. If the things he suggested didn't help, he would've had her try other things, including less expensive, less hard-on-the-body medications."

"Still, even if she'd done everything your way, maybe nothing would've gone any differently. You know that's true."

"I feel that we're going in circles, Josh. Either you get this or you don't."

"I get it more than ever, but I also have doubts that the issues are as clear-cut as you seem to think."

"It boils down to this: We don't halfway protect children because, for instance, they could be kidnapped anyway. We don't halfway teach them about God, because, you know, they could become atheists anyway. We do our best, knowing that we may not reap all the good we sow, but we have to try. Why is it okay to ignore this one area, to take it for granted? If an adult like my Daed dies young, we mourn as if God chose to take that person. But maybe it's our fault for not tending to ourselves as well as we tend to our livestock."

Joshua's cheeks burned. He felt really stupid about now, but he said nothing.

"Sorry. I shouldn't have said all that."

"Nee." He shrugged. "I see value and sound reasoning in what you're saying. Maybe you could talk with some of the founding members of different districts and get them to back you. Seems as if that would expand your reach. My family is close to numerous families and church leaders who have a lot of influence—Sam Miller, Daniel Yoder, and the Jacob Gingerich clans. All powerful Amish families." Maybe he was assuming too much. She might already have contact with people in his district and beyond. "You've clearly worked hard, and it's making a difference."

Holly took a deep breath, looking a little less upset about today's disappointment. "If I'm making such a difference, why are there not more people here? Julie thinks that maybe I offended someone who had sway over the Amish communities or that I don't actually have the bishop's support as I thought I did."

"Well . . ." Josh hated to be the one to tell her. "I think others were confused as to whether the fair was still on. I was, because I wasn't sure if what Mamm heard was true."

"If what was true?"

"She heard on the chat line that the younger Greene pharmacist canceled the fair due to Doc Lyle having a stroke."

She stared at him, disbelief radiating in her brilliant blue eyes. "He . . . what?"

10

*B*randon glanced at the Amish-made rhythm clock on the wall of the pharmacy. Four minutes after eleven. The intricately carved wooden timepiece was a gift to the store from an Amish customer years ago. Brandon had long since turned off the music function. Way back when he worked in Dad's store as a teen, the thing had driven him crazy, much to the amusement and teasing of his father, who used to sing along with it and make up words based on the task they were doing in the pharmacy. An instant of wistfulness hit him as he looked at the clock. He missed the easygoing relationship he and his dad used to have. Things had been so strained after he went to college and lost Mom. And since he'd stepped into the role of being the caregiver, their relationship was tenser than ever. Would his dad ever be fully himself again?

He should check on the fair as he had assured his dad he would. He turned to Todd. "It's a slow day. Mind if I walk down to the field and see how the fair is going?"

"Sure thing, man." Todd gestured at the stack of filled prescriptions sitting in their appropriate spot, waiting for customers to pick up the medications. "We're fully caught up. Slow day is right. I may even be able to get to your dad's never-ending to-do pile."

Thank goodness training Todd had been a breeze, as Brandon had expected. Maybe this would be the only Saturday that Brandon would have to miss his real, paying job. As part of the agreement with his dad, he'd travel back to the city on Saturdays to keep his position at BB Drugs, making it easier for the company to hire him as a pharmacist when he obtained his license.

The door chimed as he exited the store. He walked down the sidewalk toward the field and almost immediately spotted the white tops of the tents. With this beautiful day Holly should have a good turnout. What a relief he was able to convince his dad to stay home. If he could just keep the stubborn man off his feet long enough to let his body heal . . .

Holly rushed toward him.

He was about to call out "hello" when he saw her face. What was wrong? He stopped, not sure what to say.

"How could you?" Her voice shook, and her fists were clenched at her sides.

"Me? What on earth did I do?"

"You knew how much this fair meant to me! To your dad. To everyone in the whole community!"

"And?"

"How could you just cancel the fair?"

"Cancel it?"

"Ya. That's exactly what you did. The question is why. You've wasted our time, our money, and the years of trust we've been building with my district and the surrounding ones." Tears were streaming down her cheeks. "We could have saved lives today! Lives. Think about that. People who'd never seen a doctor before today or hadn't gone to one in years could've received advice that would literally have kept them alive."

"I didn't cancel the fair." He put his hands up in surrender. "I wanted to. I told my dad to, but he said no." And there was no possibility his dad had listened to him and canceled the fair. Earlier today he had made Brandon promise to attend and lend Holly a hand.

"No." Her eyes held as much accusation as anger. "*You* called the Amish chat line. *You* canceled the fair."

"I didn't." Shaking his head at her accusations, he tried to think back. "Why would I cancel it?"

"Because you don't like that your dad goes out of his way to help us. You don't want to be here, and the fair was just another item on your long list of things you'd like to put an end to."

She'd clearly picked up on his inner struggles about his dad and the Amish, feelings he'd hoped to hide from those around him. "I disagree with a lot of things concerning Dad's life, things you as the darling daughter he never had would never understand, but none of the emotional stuff between my dad and me is any of your business." Brandon drew a deep breath. "Even so, I would never, ever take it on myself to cancel one of his medical journal subscriptions, let alone something as important to him as this fair."

"Darling daughter?" She seemed completely baffled by those words. "You resent me? Me? And just how much bitterness is churning below the surface that would cause you to cancel the fair?"

"I told you I didn't do that!" As soon as the words left his mouth, he remembered being on the phone with a stranger and saying something about as far as he was concerned, it should be canceled because his dad had just had a stroke.

His words echoed in his head. *Oh no.* He closed his eyes and drew his hand down his face. He had to come clean. "Holly, I know what happened. I promise, I didn't mean to cause any confusion or mess anything up."

"What then?" She crossed her arms.

"Some man called the pharmacy the day Dad came home from the hospital, and he asked me about the plans for the fair. Moments earlier Dad almost fell and hit his head. I think you'd stepped out for some reason."

"What did you tell the caller?"

"I was upset. He insisted on speaking to me and . . ." Brandon stumbled through the rest. "I didn't know he would take my 'it should be canceled' venting as fact."

"Of course he did. You are a pharmacist with the last name Greene. The position carries power and influence."

"I haven't taken my state exams, so I'm not even licensed."

"We're Plain folk. With few exceptions no one knows or cares about your license."

Brandon clutched his forehead and sighed. *What a mess.* "How can I fix this? I'll call whoever and tell them it's my fault."

The anger finally drained from Holly's face. Instead, she just looked incredibly sad. "You can't."

"Let's reschedule. I'll help you with whatever you need." What was he saying? He already had too much on his plate. But cleaning up this mess was the right thing to do.

She looked away. "There's nothing to be done. The vendors are volunteers who had to be scheduled more than a year in advance. No one is here, and the volunteers aren't going to come back. This was my one chance to prove to them that we are interested in what they have to teach. My chance to prove that the time they took from their families to be here today was valued by the Amish community. We can't fix this."

"I'll go to each one of them and apologize then."

"Don't go to the field now and take them away from the few patients they have. You could call them later. I guess that would be a start. I'll go tell Julie what happened. She's currently teaching a diabetes class to one person."

"I'll apologize to her in person."

Holly shook her head at him as if his efforts were useless and turned back to walk toward the fair.

With his cell in hand, he walked out of the pharmacy and paused on the sidewalk. He glanced over his shoulder, making sure no one was behind him as he slowly walked and wrote the email.

From: store7006@bbdrugs.com
To: mikeprice@bbdrugs.com
Subject: Possible Acquisition
October 21, 2017

I brought to you earlier my concern about Lyle Greene of Greene's Pharmacy. He has no savings to speak of, and I'm worried about his health if he continues to work. You mentioned making him an offer to buy his store, and I think that, based on recent events, selling would be in his best interest. Please have the legal papers ready, but sit tight and keep the information quiet. I'm confident and hopeful this entire situation will end up working out for the better for everyone involved.

11

*H*olly brushed Stevie's white coat, unable to find the energy to talk to him. The day had stolen too much, and she was hiding out in the barn in no mood to talk to anyone. Waning sunlight made it increasingly difficult to see in her family's barn, a space much larger than needed for their current level of livestock. When her Daed was alive, the stalls were full. Every time she came into the barn nowadays, she recalled how they used to tend to the horses together, each loving the task of caring for their equine companions.

Stevie glanced her way while crunching his fresh hay, totally oblivious to her pain. She ran the brush over his shoulders, rubbing his muscles. He had done his part, pulling her and the rig to and from the pharmacy daily, to and from Amish homes to deliver life-saving medicines, to the health fair this morning, only to wait for her all day.

She had done her part too. She had done all she needed to organize the event, including advertising for an entire season, just like a farmer planned and planted a garden. Why had the harvest been dashed on the ground before it had a chance to ripen? She leaned her forehead on Stevie's shoulder and blinked back tears. *Surely You know the reason for all these things, God. Help me understand. Give me courage and patience.*

"Hallooooo?"

Holly jolted at the sound of her sister's voice. She stood up straight and wiped her cheeks. "Hi."

Her sister entered the barn wearing her winter coat with every button fastened. Was she that cold? She moved to the stall where Holly was, folded her arms, and propped them on the half wall. "Remember when we were little and I dressed myself?"

"What?" Why was that a topic tonight of all nights? "I guess. Maybe?"

Ivy put her chin on her folded arms. "I think I was four when Daed and Mamm decided I was old enough to dress myself. I hated the idea, completely sure I couldn't do it right. The front and back of the dresses looked the same to me, and the aprons reminded me that I needed safety pins to keep parts in place. So after dressing each morning, I'd come to you for inspection. Remember?"

The old memory stirred, and a smile tugged at Holly's lips. "Ya, I do now." She continued Stevie's rubdown, running a towel and then a brush over one section of his coat at a time.

"Each time you basically said, 'You did so well, Ivy! Come here, sweet girl, and let me help you get just a few things adjusted.' Then, while praising me for dressing myself and listing what I did right, you eased me out of the apron and dress, turned each one right side out and the front side to my front, and put them back on me. You were so affirming that I actually believed I'd done a pretty good job."

Holly chuckled. "Is there a point to this?"

"Doubtful,"—Ivy unbuttoned her coat—"except maybe you're much harder on yourself than anyone else. And God is my witness that you take life too seriously."

"Life is serious." She picked up the grooming tools and closed the stall gate behind her, leaving Stevie to his hay. "People who take it lightly are more likely to die before their time." She went to the tack room and set the tools on the bench.

"Yeah." Ivy followed her. "But with patience you can accomplish anything." Ivy peeled out of her coat. "Ta-da!" She held out her hands, showcasing an inside-out dress and apron on backward.

Holly broke into laughter.

"There she is." Ivy pointed at her, grinning. "My big sister. She's got a lot of promise when it comes to knowing when she's getting things inside out and backward. She's not there yet. But I know she can figure out life and levity and when she's taking things too hard. I'm sure of it."

"I'm not at all sure I've got anything on inside out or backward." Holly left the tack room.

Ivy picked up her coat and dusted it off. "That's what I'm here for—to let you know and to help you get it on right."

"Ya, that might mean more if you had your own clothes on right."

Ivy laughed. Holly's steps were a bit lighter as she closed the barn for the night, and they walked toward the house. Daylight saving time would end in two weeks, and when that happened, it would be dark when she arrived home from work.

"Hey, sweet girl," Mamm called as she entered the house. "I have a bowl of chicken and dumplings for you, your favorite."

"Denki." Holly's stomach ached in reaction to the smell permeating the home. She should be hungry since she'd forgotten to eat breakfast and lunch. She took off her sweater, hung it up, and walked to the kitchen. Ivy put her coat on the peg, washed her hands, and hurried into the kitchen. She pulled three bowls from the cabinet. Maybe Mamm wouldn't mind if Holly ate in her room just this once.

Mamm glanced at Ivy's inside-out clothes and didn't seem surprised. Had she seen what Ivy was up to before she left the house? "Ivy told me about today." Mamm moved closer and pulled Holly in for a hug. "I'm just so, so sorry, my Holly Noelle."

Holly closed her eyes and let her Mamm hold her and kiss her hair. If only a mother's hug and kiss could fix adult problems like they could childhood hurts. "It's okay, Mamm. At least I know how to dress myself, ya?"

Her mom released the embrace, compassion radiating in her eyes. "Some food may help a tiny bit, ya? Your sister told me that you didn't eat lunch. Come sit, eat."

So much for escaping the family interaction.

"Sorry to tell on you." Ivy dipped a ladle into the piping hot stew.

"Not a problem." Holly had to get a grip on the disappointment. But how? "It's not like that sort of thing could remain a private embarrassment. Thanks to the chat line and gossip, I'm sure everyone knows." Especially Josh. Why did he have to show up at the exact rare moment when she had no control over her emotions? Although, their conversation was perhaps the only silver lining of the entire day. Not that she had any business confiding in him. She needed to encourage him to go elsewhere for friendship.

Ivy carried a bowl into the dining room and set it on the table at Holly's place, which already had silverware, napkins, and a glass of water waiting. "The turnout was a letdown, but it wasn't a completely bad day. You'll be proud to hear that I passed my health screening with flying colors, and I won a raffle. I'm now the proud owner of a brand-new glucose meter, which I will promptly donate to someone who needs it."

"Congrats, I suppose." Holly forced a smile for the sake of her sister. In a strange way, hearing that did make her feel better. She appreciated the positivity. Did she take her job too seriously?

Her Mamm went to the counter and picked up the other two bowls. "Red gave us a call earlier when he heard about the fair. He says he wishes he could be home to give you a hug." Mamm brushed Holly's face gently with her hand as she sat down at her usual place at the table. The large wooden table had seemed particularly empty during the past few months since Holly's twenty-year-old baby brother, Ezra "Red" Zook, had been working in a different district, near the girl he was courting.

Holly sat down and bowed her head with her mother and sister. Mamm prayed out loud, thanking God for the food and praying for Holly's broken heart. Some Amish would find this tradition strange, as most prayers before meals were silent, but after Daed died, when they tried to pray silently, words bubbled up. They'd all had too many emotions to keep a family prayer time bottled up inside. She liked that their family was unique in several ways. When Mamm said "amen," Holly pulled the napkin into her lap and took several deep breaths. She dipped her spoon into the creamy, meaty broth and blew lightly on a steaming piece of chicken. They ate in silence for a few minutes, and the warmth of the broth eased her stomach.

"So,"—Mamm wiped her mouth with a cloth napkin and smiled— "while you got the horse and rig put up, your sister and I had a chance to conspire a bit."

"That's nothing new." Holly winked at Ivy. Mamm and her sister owned a cleaning and organizing business together, and to make the work go faster, they talked a large portion of the day. Thankfully for them, they never seemed to tire of each other's company.

"What would it take to schedule another fair?" Ivy asked.

Holly sighed. Did she have to rehash this? "Two things we don't have right now—time and money. I spent the budget on today's fair, and

Greene's isn't exactly raking in the big bucks these days. Neither are you two for that matter."

Mamm's and Ivy's eyes met before Ivy continued. "Why don't you come up with a concrete figure? We have some ideas."

"The first of which is a Christmas craft market," Mamm said. "Downtown Raysburg gets a lot of foot traffic during the Christmas shopping season, from Amish and Englisch crowds. I have some ideas on crafts that Ivy and I could make, and some of my friends will definitely want to make items too. Everyone could donate the crafts, and then every bit of the proceeds can go toward another community health fair event."

"That's a lot to ask others to—"

"You aren't in this alone." Ivy reached over and grasped Holly's hand, taking her by surprise. "We want to help. Let us."

Holly blinked. *You aren't in this alone.* Her sister's words reverberated in her head. For the first time since ten that morning, she felt hope start to seep back into her heart like rain into parched soil.

She took a breath, holding on to that precious feeling of optimism. She wasn't alone. Why had she let disappointment and embarrassment convince her that she was? She had her family, even with her Daed gone and her brother working in another district. This small union of Zook women was a strong and precious unit, full of love. She had support from Lyle and Julie too. With their support she would figure out a way to keep moving forward, whether rescheduling a health fair worked out or not. She even had the support of her bishop. As far as she knew, she'd be the first Amish woman in the area to get an LPN degree. She could keep that in mind and continue studying for the entrance exam.

Who knew what God had planned?

12

*B*randon walked out of the pharmacy and across the street, hoping his dad would keep his word and stay in the apartment. Mondays. His dad had a stroke on a Monday, and six months back Brandon was accused of being late to his rotation on a Monday, delaying his graduation. And today he had to apologize.

He entered the Martel Clinic, the family medical practice that often worked with his own family's pharmacy. Several Amish children were playing with blocks and puzzles in the waiting area as their mothers chatted nearby. He pulled out his phone to check the time: five minutes before noon.

Since arriving last week, he'd spoken to Julie on the phone a couple of times, conducting business between a nurse and a pharmacist. The rest of what he knew about her came from his dad. She was close to Brandon's age and had started as the nurse practitioner at the Martel Clinic last year when he was in his fourth year of pharmacy school. Since Holly was particularly upset about disappointing Julie, Brandon needed to meet with her in person. He'd called her this morning and asked if she could make time for him today, and she'd agreed to meet with him during her lunch hour.

He took a seat and watched the people around him. Two men in Plain clothes were sitting next to him, and from the bits of conversation he heard, they were discussing the ridiculousness of needing to take their medicine every day.

"Blood pressure medicine each day for the rest of my life?" an Amish man asked. "I don't feel like anything is wrong with me. Do you think it's really necessary?"

Only if you want to continue that life, Brandon thought but kept to himself.

"Don't know," the other Amish man said. "I suppose it's better than risking it. Doc Lyle will give you a good deal. I'm sure it won't be too burdensome."

Brandon tuned out the conversation. How had one comment made to a stranger during a hurried phone conversation caused such problems? And why had that Amish man on the phone taken Brandon's word as if he were in charge? Whoever the man was, he'd spread the word of cancellation far and wide. By the end of the day, only a handful of Amish people had come, ones who hadn't heard the fair had been canceled. He'd spent a good bit of the morning calling different vendors and leaving messages of apology. His dad needed a break from the pressure of the pharmacy, including health fairs, and Brandon wasn't sure why he was going through all this trouble to try to mend fences other than he felt bad for Holly. He'd never meant for her to get caught in the crosshairs of his personal frustrations.

The door to the back offices opened. "You have a good day, Amos. Remember, no lifting anything!" a gentle female voice emphasized.

An Amish man in his midfifties chuckled. One of his arms was in a sling. "I'll try, Doc."

"You get that boy of yours to move everything when you're working in your shop—even if you think you can do it. And come see me next week." A woman walked into the waiting room, her golden-brown eyes lighting up when she spotted Brandon. This had to be Julie. She pulled back the sleeve of her crisp white coat to look at her watch. "Wow, I'm actually on schedule today." She walked across the waiting area and extended a hand to Brandon. "Julie Wilson."

He shook it, noticing how pleasantly firm her handshake was, despite her soft and slender hand. "Brandon Greene."

"I figured. We haven't met in person, but I'm sure you have been told many times that you are the spitting image of your dad." She laughed and smiled in a way that eased his concern about her accepting his apology, and his mood lifted.

"Oh, I've heard that plenty. And I haven't quite decided whether it's a compliment or an insult."

She chuckled again. "Just a minute. Let me get rid of this coat, and we can go out for a quick bite. That is, if you are up for it. Or we can talk here if you'd rather. I'm just starting my break."

"Sure, let's talk over lunch." He watched as she quickly walked back behind the door to the private offices and reemerged without her white coat and stethoscope. She flipped her shoulder-length, highlighted brown hair out of her collar and smoothed her dress. Her clothing looked professional yet hinted of a style the Amish would approve of . . . for an Englisch girl.

"All right, ready." She nodded at Brandon and started for the front door. "Frances, er—my boss, Dr. Martel, likes to eat around one, so we have almost an hour. I usually go to the diner on the corner. They know me, and the price is right for almost daily lunches. Wait. You grew up here. You probably know about all the restaurants in town. Maybe I should be getting tips from you."

"I don't know about getting town info from me, but lunch at the diner sounds great." Brandon surprised himself by how much he meant it. They walked out the front door into the sunshine. Brandon knew which diner she was talking about. He had eaten there a few times as a kid and more often as a teen when working with his dad. He'd been gone from his hometown eight years, which simultaneously felt like an eternity and no time at all.

As they rounded the corner, Julie turned to him. "So what did you want to talk about? Your message was pretty vague. You concerned about your dad?"

"Well, yes, but I wanted to talk about the health fair." His cheeks felt hot in anticipation of what he was about to say. "I messed up." He quickly explained about the call and what he'd said and then glanced at Julie to see her reaction.

Her face didn't betray any anger or frustration. She nodded. "Yes, I can see someone taking the pharmacist at his word. The Amish certainly have a different view of us as health professionals than we have of ourselves. Most of them call me Doc Jules even though I'm a nurse practitioner."

"They call my dad 'doc' as well. Always have." Brandon opened the door to the diner and held it as Julie stepped through. They sat down on shiny metal stools at the fifties-style bar.

A waitress brought Julie a steaming cup of coffee and a glass of ice water. She turned to Brandon. "And you, hon?"

"Same for me, please." As the waitress left and walked over to the coffee station, he looked Julie in the eyes. "Really, I'm sorry about the fair. It was not my intent to waste anyone's time or money."

"I forgive you. I know you're going through a lot right now with your dad." She picked up a packet of sugar and shook it.

He appreciated that she didn't brush off the apology or tell him not to worry about it.

She tore open the packet and stirred the sugar into the hot coffee. "It is a setback, true, but Lyle, Holly, and I will keep trying to find ways to serve the Amish community's health needs."

"Yeah, I'm sure." He didn't know her that well, but he had no doubts that his dad and Holly would do everything in their power to serve the community—even at the expense of everything else.

The waitress returned with Brandon's drinks, took their lunch order, and left.

"How's your dad doing?"

"As well as can be expected. He hates having to rest. I need to come up with something productive he can do so he doesn't drive himself crazy."

"I can understand. He takes his work seriously."

"May I ask you a question?" Brandon hoped his inquiry wouldn't be considered prying.

"Sure."

"You seem really smart and hardworking. Why come here? Why the Amish? You aren't from this town and don't have family connections that I know of."

She nodded again. "I guess what sparked my interest initially is that I did some research on the Amish when I was in school. They are an interesting faction healthwise because they are a closed community. They have some unique genetic issues, but they lead a considerably more active lifestyle than your average American. In a way it's like looking back through time. How would our great-great-great-grandparents do if they had access to modern medicine? It's thought provoking to me."

"I guess that's interesting." He still wasn't quite convinced of the need for her to live in Raysburg.

"It's not just about a lifespan but also about quality of life." She gestured with the spoon she'd used to stir her coffee. "There's a need, especially in rural communities like this one. Frances Martel and Lyle Greene began something almost thirty years ago that was unprecedented—serving a population that had previously received very poor health care. There's no telling what the long-term outcomes will be, and I want to be a part of the ongoing process. You know, the younger generation coming in to help carry the workload. And, yes, I could work in a city and make more money and even make a positive difference in people's lives. But there is no one else out here doing what the Martel Clinic and Greene's Pharmacy are doing—putting the Plain, less advantaged folk ahead of profits."

"The problem is, if Dad doesn't start making money, I'm not sure how long he can continue to stay open." Brandon sipped his black coffee. Not the quality brew he was used to getting in the city but not bad.

The waitress arrived with their food, and they began eating.

"I've worried about that myself, to be honest." Julie wiped her mouth and took a drink. "I know only a little about the acquisition prices of drugs, but I do know that Lyle sells most of his medicines at a lower price than the chain pharmacies, and yet the chains buy in bulk, so they pay less for every drug. Added to that, Lyle often gives breaks to Amish patients who are having trouble affording their medicine."

Brandon took a drink from his mug. "He needs to scale that back a bit or at least find new ways to make money, such as getting better insurance contracts for his Englisch patients and upping his immunization rates. I don't think he actually knows about that stuff. They didn't teach those things when he was in pharmacy school. He's focused on treating patients, which is great, but he also needs to know how the new systems work in order to have a sustainable business model."

"Those are good ideas. If only he knew someone fresh out of school who could help him implement solutions like that. Maybe someone who might look a little like him. Maybe someone sitting at this counter . . ." She trailed off, grinning.

He chuckled. "Sorry, but I'm not interested, not even a little intrigued. Besides, he's very set in his ways. If he wouldn't listen to Todd ten years ago, a man he admired and once thought he wanted to take on as a partner, he's not going to listen to some greenhorn like me. And . . . I have way more school debt to pay off than I can earn in that pharmacy."

"Are your loans from the government?"

He nodded.

"Then you can apply to repay your debt based on a sliding scale. The less you make, the less the monthly payment is. From what Dr. Martel says, Todd wanted change. He wanted to veer away from helping the Amish. I think Lyle would let go of his stubbornness if he realized running things a little differently could secure the pharmacy's future."

"Maybe, but I'm not cut out for a farming community or the paycheck-to-paycheck lifestyle."

Curiosity danced in her eyes. "More a city man, huh?"

The waitress refilled their glasses, and Brandon let the conversation drop.

A couple of minutes later Julie shifted the topic to commiserating over all-night study sessions while finishing their respective degrees. Brandon offered to pay for her meal. In his mind it was part of his apology, but she declined. They paid their separate tabs and walked to the door.

"One thing about a small rural town. It doesn't have much to offer in the way of a social life. We should do this again sometime." Julie opened the front door of the diner.

Brandon took hold of the door and held it open while they both exited. She wasn't talking about a date or anything romantic, or at least it didn't seem that way to him. She was simply asking to have an enjoyable conversation over lunch as one interesting young professional to another. "Yes, we should."

When the words left his mouth, he found himself looking forward to having another lunch with her, and he realized he hadn't looked forward to anything in a long time, even something as small as a chat with a new friend. What kind of life was he building in the city if that was the case?

13

ive, ten, fifteen, twenty, twenty-five, thirty. Holly carefully counted the Zofran pills into the side of her tray, using her plastic pill-counting spatula. She scooped them back into the center of the tray and counted again. The semimundane routine tasks at the pharmacy helped soothe her worries. The failure of the health fair was sixteen days behind her, and each day brought a little more acceptance than the one before it. There *would* be other opportunities. As much as the health fair disaster had felt like the end of the world, it wasn't. She was still here working, helping.

The front door chimed as a customer entered.

"Good afternoon. Welcome to Greene's," Holly called out.

The man was about Lyle's age and had thin gray hair. He had a folder in his hand and was wearing a striped blue dress shirt and a solid navy tie. He smiled as he walked toward the prescription drop-off area. While headed her way, he glanced behind the counter. "Good afternoon, young lady. My name is David Roberts, and I'm from the Pennsylvania State Board of Pharmacy. Is Lyle about?"

Board of Pharmacy? Lyle once told her that several of his pharmacy school classmates were on the board, and since they knew him personally, they understood his regulation-abiding mind-set. So the board didn't bother to inspect Greene's often. This was her first time to see anyone from the board in Greene's Pharmacy. Was David here to check on Lyle after his stroke?

All things considered, Lyle was doing really well. Even though he'd had his stroke just three weeks earlier, he'd begun working in the over-the-counter section of the pharmacy a few days ago, albeit very slowly and carefully. No one wanted him to slow down his recovery time or risk another injury, but keeping Lyle out of his beloved pharmacy was a fight they'd lost.

Lyle walked around one of the over-the-counter shelves filled with antacid medications and came to a stop behind the man and patted him on his shoulder. "David, good to see you. It appears you've met my lead tech of ten years, Holly Zook." He looked at Holly. "David's a board inspector."

Could this visit mean they'd done something wrong? The laws for pharmacies were plenteous and strict. It came to her why he might be here. Pharmacy hours had to be listed in numerous places, the front door and online being the most common, and the pharmacy *had* to be open during those hours with a licensed pharmacist on duty. But Greene's had closed for several hours the morning of Lyle's stroke until the relief pharmacist could arrive. But surely the board could understand a medical emergency.

"Good to see you, Lyle." David smiled as he returned Lyle's shoulder pat. "Wow. You look much better than I expected."

"Thanks. I think that's a compliment." Lyle chuckled. "Hope I'm still feeling well after you tell me why you're here today. I take it this isn't a social call."

"It's not." David's smile faltered. "But nothing is going on that we can't figure out, I'm sure. Do you have a private place we can talk?"

"Absolutely. It'll be a little cramped, but let's step inside the break room." He turned to Holly. "Get Brandon, please. I want the two of you to listen to this meeting as well." He returned his attention to David. "I'm sure you understand. My memory hasn't been as reliable as I would like it to be since the stroke."

"Of course, Lyle." David motioned with his hand. "After you."

The two men went toward the break room, and Holly found Brandon sitting on a stool in the back of the prescription area, working on a stack of paperwork while muttering under his breath about insurance contracts.

"Brandon, a pharmacy board inspector is here. Your dad wants us all to meet in the break room."

"Great." Brandon sighed and pushed the stack of papers back.

It didn't sound as if he thought it was great. Were they in trouble for closing the pharmacy the morning of Lyle's stroke? Or was it something else entirely?

"Did he say why?" Brandon hopped off his stool and moved toward the gate.

Holly shook her head. "Not yet."

"Guess we'll find out."

After they entered the break room, Lyle closed the door and introduced Brandon to David. The two shook hands.

"I think the last time I saw you was when your mom and dad had me over for dinner more than two decades ago." David held his hand flat a few feet over the floor. "You were no taller than my hip." His jovial smile faded as he tapped the file in his hand, and the four of them took seats around the table. "Okay. Let's get to it. We have reason to believe Greene's Pharmacy filled five medications without prescriptions—all for the same man on the same date."

What? Holly couldn't believe it. Why would Lyle fill a medicine without a prescription? Even in an emergency situation, he could call the Martel Clinic. Doc Jules or Doc Martel would return his call, regardless of the time or day of the week.

David pulled a sheet out of the folder, but he held on to it. "We're looking at five prescriptions for one Sam Miller."

Lyle's eyes were wide. He took the paper from David and studied it, his face draining of color.

David gestured toward the sheet. "Each of the five scripts is missing the prescribing doctor's NPI number, name, and phone number, and all we have on the patient is his name."

"That's serious, Dad. I know it is." Brandon put a hand on his dad's shoulder. "But don't let it upset you. Breathe. Steady your heart. The most important thing is your health."

Holly's pulse thudded against her temples. "I'm not sure I fully understand what's going on. Everyone in the pharmacy is meticulous about logging data. Lyle has trained all of us to be that way, but what's the significance of information being missing?"

Lyle studied the paper. "The data would prove a doctor wrote the prescriptions. Otherwise it appears as if I wrote the scripts, and it's illegal for any pharmacist to write a script."

Illegal? Holly's head spun. "But how would the board get the information on that sheet? Did someone from Greene's contact them, saying this was handled illegally?" She looked from Lyle to the inspector.

"David isn't at liberty to answer that question, Holly. It's certainly possible someone from Greene's contacted him,"—Lyle tapped his fingers on the table—"especially since we have relief pharmacists working here. Harris, Todd, and Adrienne. They could've felt it was their obligation to go to the board rather than come to me."

Holly wanted to pound her fist on the table. "But whoever did this wanted to cause trouble for us. Who would go to the board rather than coming to you?" When Brandon's name came to mind, she locked eyes with him.

He held up both hands. "Why are you looking at me?"

"Holly." Lyle leaned in and put his hand over hers. "I doubt anyone's out to get us. If someone sent in a report, they were trying to do the right thing, perhaps concerned their license could be in jeopardy if they didn't report it. But a state board member has to come and inspect a pharmacy whenever the pharmacist-in-charge changes, and that happened within days of my stroke. A board member could've visited anytime in the last three weeks when we weren't in the pharmacy. Maybe the file David has is from that visit."

David cleared his throat. "All we need to focus on is finding out what happened regarding those five prescriptions. Although a board member coming to Greene's is unusual, visits like this are a normal part of pharmacy operations. Remember when BB Drugs reported you about a decade ago? They had what they thought was a false prescription that you transferred to one of their stores. I came to see you and cleared the report the same day. I hope that's the outcome today also."

Lyle set the paper on the table. "It says here I filled them on Sunday, October fifteenth." Lyle drew a deep breath and closed his eyes. "That's the day I lost."

"Lost?" David angled his head.

"Because of the stroke," Lyle clarified.

"You had the stroke *that* day?" David asked.

"No, the stroke happened the day after, but I remember nothing of the day before."

"Oh." David's eyes held concern.

Holly willed herself to sound calm. "Whether he remembers that day or not, I know that everything was handled within the legal guidelines, just like always."

David grimaced while offering a faint smile. "I'm sure. I've known Lyle since we were in college, and I know you all run a good, honest business, but the board doesn't operate on good faith. Still, we must have the hard copies of the scripts the patient brought from the doctor to prove that when Lyle filled them that Sunday, each one was legit and from a physician."

"What happens if we don't find the hard copies?" She had to ask, but surely they could find them.

"Fines and possibly a sanction," Lyle mumbled. "As much as twenty-five thousand dollars per script. But worse than the fines is a sanction, which means the pharmacy is not allowed to dispense prescriptions, and that can be anywhere from a few days to a few years."

Holly remembered the overdue bill from the medication supplier. With expenses like that, even if the sanction lasted only a few weeks, it wouldn't matter. The pharmacy would close. Who knew regulations for pharmacies were this ridiculous?

David smiled, looking sympathetic. "When everyone feels ready, I'll go with Brandon to the computer to see what a search of 'Sam Miller' reveals. Holly, you go with Lyle to the storage room and pull the printed copies of scripts for October fifteenth. Lyle will direct you from there. He knows where all the hard copies are filed."

Holly knew where they were filed too, but she wasn't going to correct him. "I'm sure this makes no difference, but with a name like Sam Miller and the fact that he came here to have a script filled, he's likely to be

Amish." She gestured toward the door of the break room. "Let's get started." Her insides were spinning like a weather vane in a windstorm, but she feigned peace.

Lyle stood, looking as uneasy as she felt. All four of them went to the gated section of the pharmacy.

David and Brandon stopped at one of the computers while Lyle and Holly went to the storage room behind the pharmacy workstation. Holly waited as Lyle unlocked the door. He flicked on the lights, revealing stacks and stacks of boxes, each holding printouts of the scripts. There were more than two years of hard copies—some from doctors' prescription pads and some digital prescription printouts—because the law required that a hard copy of the records be kept for two years.

She'd been in this room a lot over the years, filing the hard copies. It used to be easy, peaceful work, but this time the pharmacy could be at stake. What if they couldn't find the scripts? After Lyle's stroke she hadn't filed the hard copies as usual. Days passed before she caught up on her routine work, and even then she was distracted by concerns over Lyle's well-being and the preparations for the health fair. What if their search for the scripts yielded nothing and it was her fault?

She found the box marked October of this year, set it on the floor, and knelt. Lyle pulled up a step stool and sat beside her.

Sam Miller. Sam Miller. She had heard that name recently, but where? Suddenly the image came flooding back into her mind. Wet grass, a nearly empty health fair, tears, and a blond, handsome meddler named Josh Smucker listing names of influential Amish families he could reach. It was fairly likely that someone named Sam Miller in these parts was Amish. Was it possible Josh might know the right Sam Miller? And if he did, would that be useful in any way?

14

*B*randon hung up the phone. "No answer, and the voice mail was automated and full. It's possible he gave the pharmacy a number that's not his primary number. I don't understand how that's a problem when most people own a cell, but it happens too often."

David sighed and wrote down another note. After more than half an hour of running searches in the computer and making calls, Brandon struggled to hide his mounting fury from the inspector. What had Dad been thinking? Did he actually *make up* five prescriptions and give them to this man Sam Miller? It didn't sound like something his dad would've done in previous years, but it seemed that he was more willing to bend the rules when it came to his Amish patients. Did the desire to help the Amish combined with the possible mental effects of the impending stroke impede his judgment?

David clicked his pen and closed the folder. "Let's check on your dad."

Brandon went to the door of the storage room and tapped before opening it. Holly was on the floor with a large stack of printouts in her lap, and his dad was on a stool beside her.

After David entered, Brandon closed the door. "Any hard copies of the scripts?"

Holly's shoulders slumped. "No. We've looked through all of October three times, and we found nothing for a Sam Miller. You?"

Brandon shrugged. "Sort of. I found three Sam Millers in the system. Long story short, one of them came in Sunday, October fifteenth, so he's our guy. We tried the number we had on the computer for him, but no one answered, and the voice mail is full. I think he may have listed some number other than his cell phone."

David wrote down another note. "Okay, here's the deal. Because of the number of scripts and the consequences Greene's could face, it would've been ideal to find the hard copies. But if you can't come up with those, you must have proof of the scripts' validity in another way. Brandon said he would review the security footage to see if he could tell what happened to the hard copies. Hopefully, you can reach Sam Miller to find out the name of the doctor who prescribed the medicines. I feel it can be done. Apparently it'll take some time. The next board meeting isn't until December eighteenth because we aren't meeting in November, due to Thanksgiving. That gives you six weeks to find proof of the legitimacy of the scripts. Look in every corner of the store, under every desk, in every nook where small papers could've slid. Look slowly at each encounter on the security footage, searching for what may have happened. And let me know if there is anything I can do to help." He offered his hand to Lyle.

Lyle stood and shook it. "Take care, David. Can I walk you out?"

"No need." The inspector smiled and gave a small wave as he exited the cramped storage room.

Dad sank onto the stool, looking worn-out.

Once David left the room, Brandon closed the door behind him and turned around to face his dad. "Why would you fill the prescriptions with almost no info? I get that if patients are out of their maintenance medication, pharmacists often fill a day's worth to tide them over. Maybe two days' worth under the right circumstances, like the patient is traveling, or a national holiday is involved and doctors' offices are closed. But you filled five scripts for a full month's supply? Why would you do that?"

"If I could remember, I would certainly tell you. I'm sure I had a good reason." His dad stood and walked closer to Brandon. "But that aside, I want to give you a chance to tell me the truth before this investigation goes any further. Did you turn in the information about the scripts?"

What? "Are you actually going to point a finger at me, Dad?"

His dad studied him. "You're angry at having to be here, and it seems clear to me that you have little respect for my way of doing business. It's a simple question. Did you report me to try to teach me a lesson?"

"You can't mean that." The cut of his dad's accusation went deep. "I would never—"

"I hope not." His dad wouldn't meet his eyes.

Was he serious? His own son, for Pete's sake! "Is there anyone you trust besides Holly?" He raked his hands through his hair. "Man, alive! You two are something else. Both of you accusing me. First her staring at me with an accusatory look when David was here, and now you. Her dad died, and you took her under your wing, made a position for her, and trained her, watching after her as if she were your own. Mom got sick, and other than allowing a few visits, you insisted I stay at college so I didn't get behind. And when Mom died, you made me return to school two days after the funeral."

Both Holly and Dad were staring at him.

Brandon had their attention, and he would use the opportunity. "I would never do what you're accusing me of. If I had realized scripts were missing, I would've come to you, and we'd have launched a search, tearing this place apart until we found the hard copies. But the fact that you pushed me to stay away, and then when I do come home, you and Holly doubt me is extremely disturbing."

"Wait." Holly stepped in closer, staring into his eyes as if looking for something. "Lyle, tell him how much you missed him."

Dad said nothing.

Typical.

Holly's eyes brimmed with tears as she turned to his dad while pointing at Brandon. "Tell him how often you picked up the phone, intending to ask him to come home and then changed your mind and hung up." She nodded at Brandon. "Time and again before your mom passed and that first year after she died, I saw him with that phone in his hand, shaking and teary eyed, wanting to ask his only child to come home. But he didn't for your sake, not his. He would say, 'He's building a life of his own, and I won't interfere with that. His mom told me before she died that she didn't want him giving up his future because it was her time to go home.'" Holly moved to Dad. "Lyle, tell him."

But his dad stared at the stacks of boxes. Was Holly seeing a part of his dad that Brandon had missed?

Brandon angled his head to get a better look at his dad's face. "Dad, is that true?"

His dad gestured toward the boxes. "Believe what you want. We have work to do."

"Dad." Brandon couldn't hide his disbelief. Was his dad really that apathetic about their relationship? "Nothing is more important than what's taking place right now between us. Come on. You know that."

His dad didn't budge for several seconds. Finally he nodded and got up from the stool. His hazel eyes met Brandon's. Memories of him as a young man pounded Brandon. Thoughts of his dad spending hours throwing him the football, pitching him baseballs, or going swimming with him every weekend rolled through Brandon, but it was a gray-haired old man who inched his way forward.

"It's true, Son. How could either of us doubt the other one?" His dad embraced him, holding on for nearly a minute.

The warmth of his father's embrace eased the sadness and anger that had been building inside him for years. It felt as if a dam burst, freeing a river of love and forgiveness. How had Brandon held it in so long? The relief was staggering. Both of them were sniffing and wiping their eyes when they let go.

Holly chuckled and moved to Brandon until the toes of her shoes were inches from his. She once again gazed into his eyes. "I'm sorry for all the misunderstandings and for accusing you."

"I'm not the enemy." He never wanted to seem like one.

"I know. You're the opposite." She grabbed his hand. "Forgive me, please?"

He looked at his dad. "You know, I would've adjusted easier to having a little sister if you and Mom had ever informed me that I had one."

Lyle chuckled. "Put it on the list of things I should've handled better, and maybe one day I'll admit to it."

Holly smiled up at him, and when Brandon returned her smile, she hugged him. "Family fights. They're just so much fun, right?"

Brandon returned the hug. "No, but they do clear the air a bit."

"Son, I accused you because I don't know you anymore, not really, and that's my fault. I've let too many years go by with barely seeing you, and then I looked at your frustration about having to be here. I assumed too much and shared too little."

"It's my fault too. You did assume too much. After Mom died, I hated returning to college, but once I settled in there, I didn't want to come home. I missed Mom too much, and it was easier staying there and being super busy. So I'm just as culpable for the distance between us." Brandon clicked his tongue. "When the Greene men get things wrong, we don't do it halfway, do we?"

His dad chuckled. "Apparently that's quite true."

Brandon and his dad remained in place, smiling. Then Brandon's face fell, and he shifted as the reality of what they currently faced crashed in. "This would be a perfect moment except we have a very serious situation that needs our attention."

Holly set the stack of printouts in their box. "We need to find this Sam Miller. Since none of the contact info we have works, we're going to need a different plan for locating him. I suspect he's Amish, but it would help if we knew what Sam looked like. Can we skim the security tapes from that Sunday?"

"Yeah, sure." Brandon went to a tiny desk in the corner of the room to access the computer that stored the security footage. He sat in the straight-backed chair and started typing. Dad and Holly watched over his shoulder as he pulled up the footage for that Sunday. He fast-forwarded to the hours the store was open, and then he slowed the speed of the footage but still moved faster than real time.

Holly grabbed his shoulder. "Stop. Right there."

Brandon paused the footage. A man wearing a straw hat and suspenders stood at the counter. He had several prescription bottles in his hands but not in the exact style as Greene's. Brandon would bet they were empty vials from a different pharmacy. But when Dad refilled them, why hadn't he saved the bottles or at least the labels from the bottles?

"I think we're looking at our Sam Miller," Brandon said.

"He *is* Amish." Holly pointed at the screen. "There's no way an Amish man would purchase anything on a Sunday unless he had no other choice."

Dad put a hand on Brandon's other shoulder. "The scripts are all heart meds, so if the patient had run completely out, that would be an acceptable emergency to any Amish person."

Brandon enlarged the view of the man. "We can look at him from various camera angles, but I doubt we'll be able to see his face under that broad-brimmed straw hat." He looked up at Holly. "Do you know any Sam Millers?"

"I don't, although it seems as if I should." She stared at the computer screen. "I've been thinking about it though, and I know someone who knows at least one Sam Miller." She leaned in. "I can't see the man's face, but the way he carries himself, he appears to me to be middle aged. He doesn't have a beard, which means he's single." She stood straight. "There was an Amish guy at the health fair—Josh—and he mentioned that name. Maybe God is at work in this, helping Greene's Pharmacy to stay alive."

"We all hope that," his dad said.

"We do." Brandon had never cared more about this pharmacy than now. It wasn't his personal dream, but it was his dad's, his mom's, and now Holly's, and that was enough. He turned off the screen and stood. "Here's the plan. We are going to move forward under the assumption that these are legal prescriptions and that something happened to prevent Dad from getting them transferred into our computers properly. And that there was a good reason for Dad to fill the whole prescription rather than just give a small supply to get him through to Monday, when the doctors' offices opened back up."

"I like the sound of that," Dad said.

"Me too." Holly smiled.

Brandon nodded. "I'll try to track down the doctor. I'll call all the practices I can and ask if they have a patient with the name Sam Miller, starting nearby and expanding the radius. There's no telling where in the country he originally obtained the prescriptions, but it's more likely that he saw a doctor in Pennsylvania or a neighboring state. Dad, you need to send a courier to the address we have for Sam Miller. See if anyone lives at that address. And keep trying the phone number. Maybe eventually someone will answer. We'll look through the security footage from Sunday and the surrounding days to see if any leads turn up concerning what could have happened to the hard copies or at least the old prescription bottles or labels. Holly, you talk with Josh and then make calls, getting a phone number or address for every Sam Miller you can. But remember the HIPAA privacy rules."

Brandon hoped this plan worked, because he was sure it would break his dad and Holly if the pharmacy went under.

15

*J*oshua stood inside the phone shanty, the handset balanced between his face and shoulder. He took a breath and dialed the number to Greene's Pharmacy. It rang twice before someone answered.

"Greene's Pharmacy. Holly speaking." Her voice seemed pleasant, but her words came out quick. He could hear her clicking away, probably on a keyboard. Yesterday she'd left a message for him on the answering machine, but she'd sounded flustered and had stumbled over her words.

"Hi, Holly. This is Josh. I got your message about your pharmacy and Sam Miller." The first time he met Holly at the gatherings, he had introduced himself as Josh instead of the usual Joshua, trying to sound more casual, more relaxed. Now she was the only person who called him Josh.

"I'm so glad to hear from you!"

He felt his cheeks flush, although he knew her excitement wasn't directed at him personally. She just needed his help. How many times did he have to remind himself that she wasn't interested? "Good."

Part of him wanted to keep interaction with her to a minimum. If he just asked his parents the question and passed the information to her, he could be done. But his parents were likely to remember more helpful information if they talked to her themselves.

He leaned against the phone shanty as he drew a breath. "I've been thinking about your message, and you need to talk to my parents face to face. They know a lot of people, but it'll take a good conversation with them to be sure you get all you need."

"That would be wonderful. I mean, I'm not expecting a miracle. I know 'Sam Miller' is a common name, but maybe, just maybe, I could get a lead on him through your family's contacts."

"Ya, maybe so. My folks are sort of the cornerstones of the Amish in this area, so they know everyone." He sat in the folding chair.

"That's great. If possible, talking to them sooner is better than later." She sounded a bit unsure of herself, which wasn't very Holly-like.

"Today would work for us."

"Really? That's short notice for your folks."

"They won't mind. I'm sure of it." Mealtime conversations were often best for exchanging information in a slow, methodical way, so it made sense to invite her to eat with them. But the words stuck in his mouth.

She continued clicking on something in the background. "I'm sure I can get one of our regular drivers to bring me your way. What time would work best?"

Speak, Joshua. A little hope—and a whole lot of reluctance—nibbled at him. "Come as soon as you're able. How about eating dinner with us? Say five thirty? By the time we finish our desserts, you should know all they have to share on the topic."

"Denki." She breathed deeply, sounding relieved and grateful. "I'll be there. Denki, Josh."

What time was it now? Based on the sun's position, he'd guess around four. "Ya." He just hoped that being a nice guy didn't backfire. *"Gern gschehne."*

"See you then."

As he heard her hang up, he realized he was smiling, despite his reluctance and his earlier warnings to himself. He stood and wiped the grin from his face with his hand. It was just a work thing for her. It wasn't like she wanted to meet his parents in order to date him. He placed the receiver on its rest and exited the phone shanty.

A few chickens squawked at him from behind their fence as he lightly jogged to the farmhouse. He crossed the weathered porch and entered through the bright blue door. One of his nieces had painted it the last time she visited, attempting to bring a little pep back to the old white farmhouse. Something smelled delicious, most likely bread baking. As much as his mouth watered at the aroma, he worried that his Mamm wasn't taking her new dietary recommendations seriously enough. She was in a chair at the table, rolling dough into dinner rolls.

"Hallo." He kissed her on the cheek. "I called Holly back. She's coming for dinner around five thirty. Sorry for the short notice."

She waved off the apology with flour-covered hands. "It sure took you long enough, but I had a good feeling about that one after you mentioned her several months back." Mamm had the smile of a serene barn cat as she continued rolling the dough.

"No." He tapped the table. "Uh, no." He sat across from her. "I already told you and Daed that she just needs help finding an Amish man who picked up a prescription at Greene's."

"Of course." She winked at him. "Don't worry. I had a good feeling about your returning that call, and I was already making something special."

Joshua eyed his Mamm. It was clear she hadn't taken him seriously when he said Holly was coming only for work-related reasons. But even though Holly was coming to find info for the pharmacy, she'd probably take time to give Mamm more advice on how to manage her diabetes. So the visit would be beneficial for him and his parents, but he was sure to be ribbed the whole time about having a girl over. "Daed outside?"

"Ya, he's checking on *da Bobbelis.*"

"They're growing fast." He really needed to get back to work and help his Daed check on the baby chickens, but the desire to sneak a few extra minutes with his Mamm since her diagnosis was undeniable. "Hopefully they'll be strong enough before it gets freezing cold."

"If anyone can make those chicks survive our winter, it's you and your Daed."

"Hope so." He ran his fingers across the edge of the flour on the table, pushing it back toward her. "Listen, about tonight's meal—don't exert yourself."

"I'm fine. I fix dinner every night. I've already started it, and having one more person won't be any harder."

Was that supposed to make him feel better? To tell the truth, he wondered if Daed and he took her for granted. "Okay, but let me know if you need help with anything for tonight." He rose and went out the back door, heading toward the chickens and his father.

Since the start of November, the number of farmers' markets that Joshua had attended to sell eggs had dropped substantially. That left the normal upkeep and egg-gathering chores and of course the new chicks.

He grabbed the measuring tape and a few metal poles to continue the project of the day: expanding the area of the yard for the young chickens that would soon need more space. He'd started this morning and then stopped at midday to have a bite of food with his parents before he began cleaning the lining of the chicks' pens. The time passed quickly. Too quickly. It wasn't until his stomach growled that he realized it had been an hour since Holly had called and it was nearing suppertime.

A quick sniff let him know his clothes stank. Also, Mamm might need a hand with dinner, so he hurried inside to grab a shower. In no time he was turning off the shower, smelling and feeling much more human. Steam rolled through the bathroom as he dried off and dressed. What time was it anyway? Buttoning his shirt, he headed down the stairs. Halfway down he heard his Daed's voice coming through an open window in the kitchen. *Uh-oh.* Had Daed been the one to greet Holly in the driveway?

Joshua went to the front door and opened it, intending to politely interrupt his Daed's sure-to-be-embarrassing storytelling session, but where was he? Joshua stepped onto the porch and saw his Daed in the yard, at the corner of the house. With Holly. Of course.

Her eyes met his with a look that seemed to indicate amusement. But she was here on business. Had Daed let her ask anything important, or had he just launched into storytelling mode?

His Daed laughed. ". . . and then, whoosh, he cleared the fence but accidentally landed in a giant mud puddle. Unfortunately for his sister, who had been watching from a place of supposed safety, mud splattered all over her newly sewn dress." Daed made a splashing motion with one hand and then gestured for Holly to go toward the steps to the house. Joshua returned to the front door and opened it, and she gave a little wave as she passed him. She probably would've spoken except Daed was still talking.

Joshua rubbed the back of his neck. "Daed, I don't think she needs to hear any more about that story."

"Oh, the legend of Carlton, the original grumpy mule, definitely needs to be spread." Daed grinned. "As well as your heroic escape from his wrath."

Joshua chuckled. "That mule died years ago."

"Ya, but his infamy never will," Mamm piped in as they entered the kitchen.

He looked from his Mamm to his Daed. They appeared to be suppressing smiles and giggles and were failing. And now he was smiling too.

Even with all the teasing they gave him, he loved seeing their bond. They had a lifetime of stories, memories, and exploits from farm life and raising thirteen kids.

"Holly, meet my parents, Edith and Albert, very serious pillars of the community." Joshua gestured to them while shaking his head. They had enthusiasm for life and especially for each other. He wanted to make sure that Mamm made her health a top priority so she and Daed could have as many years together as possible.

"We're so glad to have you over." Mamm set a pan on the stove, gave Holly a hug, and stepped back. "About time our youngest brought a girl home."

And there it was. Despite his warnings, Mamm was going to act as if this were a first date.

Holly laughed as if she was taking everything his parents said as complete jesting. *Good.* "Denki for having me, Edith. It's nice to meet you in person. I can't tell you how much I appreciate your family's help. How have you been feeling?"

"Much better, liewi. I'll get this diabetes routine down. Dinner is ready. Are you hungry?"

Holly put her hand on her stomach for a moment. "Very."

"Gut. Sit while I move the food to the table."

"I'll do no such thing. I insist on helping." Holly washed her hands. Joshua and his Daed stayed out of the way while the two women poured drinks and filled the table with Mamm's rolls he had smelled earlier, her salisbury steak, maple-glazed carrots, and Parmesan potatoes. How had Mamm pulled this off in such a short time? This was a step up from their typical fare.

Mamm ushered the group to sit down, and they bowed their heads for the silent prayer.

Afterward Mamm leaned toward Holly. "I'm so glad you're here. It's been a while since we had a young visitor. All of our older children are married and have lives of their own in other districts. This one, however,"— she pointed at Joshua—"has never shown much interest in socializing. But one night he came home after a gathering and just couldn't stop talking about this girl he'd met named Holly. Keep in mind it's pretty unusual for our youngest to have much to say about anything. We knew this had to be one special girl."

Joshua nodded, hoping his face didn't reflect the embarrassment his Mamm's words caused. They were true, and Holly knew it, but did his Mamm have to talk about it *with* Holly? "I'm sure Holly knows she's a fine young woman. But remember, she's here to learn about every Sam Miller you and Daed can think of. I was also hoping she could chat with you about some of the lifestyle changes the doctor suggested to manage your diabetes."

Holly reached for her cup of water. Did she feel as uncomfortable as he did? If so, she didn't show it. "Good suggestion, Josh." She took a sip of water. "Edith, can you tell me what instructions the doctors had for you?"

Thank goodness for a new subject. Holly spent several minutes listening to Mamm's answer, and then she shared some easy ways to implement better food choices in their daily meals and simple ways to keep her blood sugar from being on a roller coaster. Joshua appreciated the tidbits . . . and that the new subject made things feel less strained.

Daed dipped seconds onto his plate. "Joshua said you're looking for an Amish man named Sam Miller."

"I am, ya." She glanced at him.

Mamm wiped the corner of her mouth with a napkin. "You couldn't find a more common name, especially around here."

Holly's eyes met his, and he saw concern.

He focused on his parents. "But you guys can come up with a list of Millers, and that would be a start for her, right?"

"Sure." Daed nodded. "We can make a list. It'll be a long one, but the good news is that even if the right Sam Miller doesn't make it onto the list, he's very likely to be related to someone who is on it—simply because he's Amish and has the last name Miller. But I don't think having the list will solve all the issues. Not all Amish in this area have a phone shanty, much less a cell number. Even if they did, we don't have everyone's number."

"True." Mamm narrowed her eyes, clearly mulling on that. She gasped. "*Ach,* you know what? There's a fall festival this weekend not more than a few miles from here. It'll be smack in the middle of Amish Miller country. That event would be a good place for Joshua and you to walk around and talk to any Sam Millers there."

"A fall festival with Millers? That sounds great." Holly sat up a little straighter. "She's volunteering you, Josh."

"So I heard." Joshua was caught with no way to decline. "Not a problem." Except everyone he knew would assume he and Holly were dating, and then she'd find her Sam Miller and be on her merry way.

Holly drew the glass of water to her lips and lingered there for several long moments. "That's a great idea . . . if I haven't located the right man by then."

"If I knew a little more about why you're looking for a Sam Miller," Daed said, "I could make some phone calls and ask some questions. Seems like that would at least get you pointed toward the right Miller family."

"A list would be fantastic, and I appreciate your offer to make calls. Unfortunately, privacy laws won't allow me to tell you anything specific, such as his health issues or what medication he picked up. We can't even tell someone who isn't Sam Miller why we're looking for him. If we're talking to a Sam Miller, we can ask if he visited Greene's Pharmacy on Sunday, October fifteenth. If he didn't, we thank him for his time and move on. No elaboration or speculation allowed."

"Ach, I've had to sign those papers . . . What are they called?" Mamm pursed her lips.

"HIPAA."

"Ya, that's it. I've signed a lot of them, but I had no idea about the laws behind that thin slip of paper."

Holly nodded. "The laws are there to protect people, and I believe in them, but in this instance it's making things difficult."

"It won't be too difficult." Mamm clasped her hand over Holly's. "We'll make it a team effort. If you and Joshua do the dishes, Albert and I will go to our bill-paying desk and look for phone numbers and addresses of every Sam Miller we know." Mamm eyed him, and Joshua knew she was excited to help . . . and perhaps even more thrilled at the prospect of getting Holly and him working side by side without anyone around.

Joshua's chest felt a little funny. Was that hope or dread?

Holly beamed, taking a moment to look at each of them. "I can't tell you how much this means. This pharmacy is everything to me. If this mystery isn't solved, its fate will be in jeopardy. Until now I've felt powerless. Denki."

Her smile was as if the sun had come out after a bleak winter, and the joy of it rushed through him.

How could he be around her and keep the level head he needed?

16

The sounds of children laughing and adults chatting filled the air, and Holly breathed in the aromas of the fall festival. The buttery-sweet scent of kettle corn blended with the earthy smells of fresh hay and fallen leaves. A dozen Amish children were lined up for the horse-pulled hayride, almost bouncing in anticipation. But she and Josh weren't here to partake of the festivities. He stood nearby, talking with one of the Millers. It was clear to her this was not the lead they were looking for. So why hadn't Josh brought this conversation to a close already?

"Well." The middle-aged Amish man folded his arms across his chest. "I'm Simon Miller, but I got a cousin named Sam Miller. Everyone says he's my spitting image, so I understand the confusion." The man scratched his head through his straw hat. "His son is Samuel Jr., but he's only nine, so I doubt he's your guy. And come to think of it, I got at least one other Sam Miller, my great-uncle, but he goes by 'Sammy' on account of not getting confused with his father, who was also Samuel Miller, but he passed about two decades ago, so I don't think he's your guy either."

"Definitely not." Josh made a few notes on a small notepad. "I appreciate that you mentioned him." He tapped the pen against the paper. Holly wanted to grab his arm and move on. How did Josh have patience to linger like this? "So the Sam Miller who is your cousin and the Sammy Miller who is your great-uncle—do you have their addresses or numbers for a phone shanty where we can reach them?"

"Not off the top of my head. My cousin lives about a hundred and fifty miles from here in Maryland."

Josh took a deep breath and let it out. "Any chance he was visiting last month?"

"Well, I don't think so. At least if he did, he didn't tell me, which would be quite unusual as he is really fond of my wife's apple pie, and it is apple season right now. Secret family recipe on her side."

"Sounds like a smart man." Josh grinned. "And your great-uncle?"

Simon Miller chewed his lip. "Well, I haven't seen him since last year. He has trouble getting out of his house, you see. Bad leg."

Josh nodded. "So he probably didn't walk into Greene's Pharmacy."

Simon's eyes flashed as if he'd remembered something. "Hey, you know what? Usually this fall festival is the only annual event the family has, but there will be a whole bunch of Millers gathering for my grand-parents' seventy-fifth anniversary. Noah and Rachel Miller. Why don't you come by? I bet you'll meet several Sams. There's even a Samantha."

A desire to holler in victory rushed through Holly. Josh's patience had just paid off. Big-time. "Well, denki, Simon." Josh glanced at her, an endearing smile on his face. "That could be very helpful. Where's the gathering?"

"Not too far from here, over in New Springs on November eighteenth."

November eighteenth? That was next weekend. What a gold mine to have learned that piece of information.

As Simon gave the full address, Josh wrote it down, and then he closed the notepad. "Thank you so much, Simon. It was good to meet you." The men shook hands.

"It's no trouble at all. You tell your Daed I said hello."

"Of course. Take care." Josh nodded goodbye and motioned for Holly to walk with him. When they were out of earshot of Simon, Josh whispered, "If I ever have kids of my own, I'm naming each one something unique."

Holly couldn't help but laugh. "No more Joshua Smuckers?"

"Sadly one of my many nephews is already named after me. I better tell him to go by Joe or something else if he ever goes to the pharmacy. Avoid a mix-up."

"The issue we're having with Sam Miller has never happened before with anyone, not in the whole history of the pharmacy. We fill hundreds of scripts accurately every week, and we ask for way more information than just the patients' first and last names. Send us ten Joshua Smuckers, and I guarantee we'll keep them straight." She put her hands on her hips, refusing to smile as she mocked setting him straight. "Now, come again?"

He put his hands up in surrender. "Only teasing. For sure, there's no mistaking your identity, Holly Noelle. Your siblings have Christmas-sounding names too, don't they?"

She grinned as they strolled through the festival, apparently on their way back to Josh's rig. "Ya, Christmas was kind of my parents' theme. Mamm went into labor with me on Christmas Day, and I was born a day later."

"You were born on Second Christmas?"

"I was. My sister, Ivy, was born almost two years later on December twenty-first, and my brother, Red, was born two years after that on December twenty-ninth. Though technically he's named after my Daed, Ezra. I was born at home, and because of the holiday, my parents had a lot of extended family visiting, all waiting in anticipation for me, the firstborn of my parents' relatively new marriage. They had married ten months earlier. The story is that after recovering from the daylong birthing process, my Mamm and Daed paraded me, all swaddled tight, and placed me on blankets on the table in the center of the Christmas wreath, among all the decorated foods and Christmas cards. It's why my community still calls me Holly Noelle, though I prefer just Holly." She smiled, remembering all the times her Daed had told the story.

Josh beamed back at her. "That's quite the birth story." He shrugged. "I don't have any stories that interesting. I'm afraid that by the time I came along as kid number thirteen, my parents pretty much put a basket in my hands immediately and said, 'Go to work and help your siblings gather eggs.' Not a lot of excitement there."

Holly pointed at him. "I don't believe that for a second. I saw how your parents fussed over you."

He laughed. "I was kind of blocking that out and hoping you'd forgotten."

"No such luck, Joshua Smucker the first."

He groaned while still chuckling. "You'd have to go back at least two hundred years, maybe two thousand, to find the first Joshua Smucker."

"True. And we might need to travel to Europe to figure out if that name crossed over with the Amish or if it began in America." She snapped her fingers. "Add it to our list, Josh."

She'd meant it to be funny, but he glanced at her, looking a bit confused.

You are here to work, Holly. But it was so easy to fall into joking and laughing with him. Still, it wasn't right or fair to behave as if she were open to dating him. She could never be available for more than friendship.

But Josh needed to find someone, and suddenly a solution sprang to mind. Since he got along with her, he would get along with Ivy. And he'd mentioned being interested in music. That would go great with Ivy's annual caroling project, which she would start soon.

They climbed into the rig. Taking the reins, Josh turned to her. "So you want to resume our Sam Miller list by following some leads on Monday evening?"

"Actually, I was wondering what you were doing on Sunday evening. My sister, Ivy, is starting caroling practice for this year, and she could really use a strong male voice. If I'm recalling right, you're a musician."

"Well, as much of a musician as one can be while tending chickens all day and living in a community that forbids musical instruments. But, ya, I do enjoy singing. That sounds like fun." He smiled at her before looking away, cheeks a bit flushed.

Despite herself, she could feel heat creep up her own cheeks. For both their sakes, he needed to connect with Ivy.

17

*B*randon was on hold with yet another doctor's office trying to reach any doctor who might have seen a Sam Miller. Thank goodness the full stringency of the HIPAA laws didn't prohibit communication between a patient's pharmacy and the doctor's office. This was the fifteenth office he'd tried this week. Finally the bland on-hold music stopped, and the line clicked.

"This is Nikki, Dr. Smith's nurse. I was looking in our computer system, and it appears we do have a patient named Sam Miller."

Thank You, God. "Excellent. The receptionist may have told you, but this is Brandon over at Greene's Pharmacy in Raysburg, Pennsylvania. I need to know if Dr. Smith prescribed five different heart medications for Mr. Sam Miller. Our pharmacy is missing some information on the prescriptions." Brandon readied a pen to write down anything she might tell him, hoping she would confirm this was the right patient.

"Oh, hmm. I'm not seeing any information that this Mr. Miller is on any heart meds. What's his birthday? We may be talking about a different patient."

Brandon sighed. Of course. "I'm afraid that is part of the info we're missing. This Sam Miller is probably around fifty, and he's Amish."

"I'm sorry. I'm afraid we must be talking about a different patient. I saw our Mr. Miller two weeks ago. He is definitely not Amish. Are you sure you have the right practice?"

"No, unfortunately I'm not." Brandon stifled a scream of frustration.

"Oh. Well . . . good luck with what you're looking for." *Click.*

Apparently even chipper nurses had a limit to their patience, not that Brandon could blame her. He was annoyed too.

He hung up the phone and glanced at the clock. Four o'clock. Holly was still at some Amish fall festival looking for Sam Miller. Luckily they had Sandy, their part-time tech, who was reasonably fast, and of course Todd, who had years of experience on the bench. The pharmacy didn't seem behind. He logged off the computer, and then a random thought struck. Maybe in his dad's confusion he had put a note in that day's financial ledger instead of the proper place. Brandon headed toward the storage room.

He walked into the small room, pulled out the large finance book, and set it on the desk. He flipped through it until he found October, which was toward the end of the large tome. No notes appeared to be tucked in the book as he turned the pages, but a number in red ink jumped out at him at the bottom of October's financial overview.

That can't be right. He can't be that far behind. He flipped back to September, then August, then July. Each month the pharmacy was barely breaking even. How on earth could Greene's be so busy and so unprofitable?

He closed the book and tucked it under his arm and then headed up the stairs to look for his father. He knocked and opened the door. "Dad?" Brandon called out, entering the apartment.

"Back here, Son."

He followed the sound of his dad's voice to the small "office" that was mostly filled with aging books on pharmaceutical studies and outdated business practices. Dad had apparently been on the phone, and he put the cordless handset for the home line back in its base.

Dad grimaced. "I was calling a few other pharmacies in our area to see if they had filled anything for our patient. Nothing."

"Yeah, same here. I'm afraid I had no success in finding Sam's doctor today."

"I'm sorry. I can't tell you how embarrassed I am about this whole thing." He leaned back in the creaking leather chair. "Today I also started the process of filing to get some extra security footage from a third-party company. They put their cameras in the pharmacy a few months ago, but I let the contract lapse last month. It's lots of paperwork, and it may not lead to anything."

Brandon wasn't sure whether to step inside the office or wait at the door. "I'm sure we'll figure out what happened. Maybe Holly was successful today. But I wanted to ask you about something else. I had an idea that maybe the missing script note was filed in the wrong place, so I opened your financial ledger."

His father groaned. "I really wish you hadn't. The pharmacy's finances are my business."

Brandon walked forward and placed the book in front of his father. "Look, you want Greene's Pharmacy to meet the needs of this community, but I'm concerned you aren't modernizing in ways that could help you stay open."

"If modernization means not taking care of my patients, then I'm not interested. I'll find a way to stay open."

"While making no headway toward saving for retirement? That's not okay, Dad. I'm not talking about getting rid of your Amish patients or even charging them more. The other day I used the pharmacy's log-in info to look at the official CMS.gov site, and Greene's has only three of five stars. The good news is the public can't see that. It's only for insurance companies, the government, and professionals within the industry. Remember that your rating determines how much the insurance companies can charge you to keep your insurance contracts every month. A bad rating can cost even a small pharmacy more than six figures in a year."

Dad waved his hand as if to dismiss the notion. "I don't have time to keep up with the games the politicians dream up. Stars. Sounds like those video games you used to play when you were a kid. It'll be something different soon enough."

"Maybe. But until then you really should keep up with these things. Right now you're losing money on every Medicare script you fill. Those patients make up a large portion of your non-Amish customers."

"And you know how to get that rating up?"

"I have some good ideas of where to start. For one, when you give medicines away, you still have to document it for the insurance companies. Otherwise, they think the patients aren't taking their meds every month, and you get dinged on compliance. Also, when was the last time you gave an immunization?" Brandon started to cross his arms, but he lowered them, hoping to keep his posture humble.

The last thing he wanted to do was come across as if he thought he was a better pharmacist. He wasn't for a lot of reasons, starting with the fact that he would never have his dad's dedication or stamina to give so selflessly. But his dad was lacking in areas that were Brandon's forte. Dotting i's and crossing t's to satisfy the higher-ups came naturally for him, which was good, because corporate pharmacists daily dealt with long lists of such matters.

Dad shrugged. "Most people would rather their doctor immunize them."

"Some. But you have the potential of making good money offering flu shots for your insured patients."

"Brandon, don't you think we have enough going on right now with this lost information? Can this stuff wait?"

"That's the problem. When you run a pharmacy, there are always issues that come up. You need to make time to look at this with me."

"You win. I will. Soon."

Brandon stifled a sigh. *Soon, later—same thing, Dad, and it means not now, which means never.* "Okay. Do you need anything?"

"Haven't I seemed capable of taking care of myself over the last few weeks? I'm good. I'm going to make a few more phone calls."

Brandon nodded and exited the room, leaving the money ledger on the desk and closing the door behind him. Though they had made real progress in their relationship, the old strain was still there. If only he could come up with a good plan to help his dad understand modern pharmacy practices. Maybe Mila would have some ideas. He pulled out his cell, went to Favorites, and pushed her name, which was the top entry.

"Heeey!" She sounded rather high spirited. The background noise made it seem as if she was standing in the wind.

"Hey, what are you up to?" Brandon smiled, thinking of her long hair blowing in the wind.

"Impromptu road trip." He heard a female voice giggling in the background. "Katy and Laura from school sprang it on me. It's my three-day weekend off. That must sound like a foreign language to you."

"Yeah. Look, do you have a minute to talk, or can you call me back later?"

"It's really hard to hear you right now, and calling later will be hard to do tonight. We're going to a newly opened restaurant and then a country music concert. Katy even brought me a cowboy hat." More giggling. "I would have invited you, but I already knew what your answer would be."

"True. We can talk later. Have fun."

"I'll call you tomorrow." The phone beeped as the call cut off.

He lowered the phone, staring at it. If they actually managed to talk tomorrow, he'd be surprised. Whenever one of them called to talk, the other one was too busy. That's how it'd been for the last two weeks. He was beginning to think that wherever he was, he didn't fit—not here in work-hard-for-no-money Raysburg or in the carefree lifestyle Mila had built for herself in the city.

Feeling rather displaced, he shoved the phone into his pocket. He needed a walk.

18

*J*oshua lifted his voice to sing the countermelody of the chorus of
"The First Noel" and was satisfied that he'd hit the right notes,
making a pleasant harmony with the melody most of the carolers were
singing.

"Noel, Noel, Noel, Noel, born is the King of Israel."

"Excellent job, Snow Buntings!" Ivy clapped her hands. Earlier when
she was stepping onto a wooden box that appeared to have once held
vegetables, she explained that she needed to stand there so everyone
could clearly see her hand motions and so she could make eye contact
as needed. The small singing group of about fifteen was arranged on
benches in what was usually a craft shop, with the large tables pushed
aside to make room.

"Do we have to be called the Snow Buntings?" a male voice called
out. Snickering followed.

"Ya, we do. I'm the leader, so I get to pick. Our youth group is the
Finches, and snow buntings are also songbirds, but that name gives us a
Christmasy feel."

Another singer groaned, and several more laughed.

Ivy held her hands up to call the group to order. "Josh, thanks for
doing that part I asked you to sing. You'll have to teach the rest of the men
that part."

"Sure," he mumbled, not caring much for the attention of the entire group on him. Ivy had asked him to sing the countermelody, but he didn't count on her drawing attention to him about it. He glanced over to the women's section of the choir. Where did Holly go? When he'd arrived, he'd spotted her across the room. Their eyes had locked, and she smiled, but all they managed was a wave before Ivy brought the gathering to order, putting the men on one side and the women on the other.

"Very gut." Ivy smiled as she lowered her arms from directing the singers. "This may be the best-sounding group of carolers we've had yet." Ivy squinted, looking at a clock on the far wall. "Ach. Sorry. I've run thirty minutes past when I said I would end the practice, so that's it for today. Thanks for coming. You can stack your lyric sheets on this crate. Remember, the weekly singles singing for tonight is at Amity's home in about . . . ten minutes. See you all next week!" She hopped off her crate.

The singers started chattering among themselves as they made their way toward the door and stacked their papers as instructed. Joshua hung back, waiting for the room to clear so he could talk to Ivy. This was a good place for caroling practice. There were several long tables that were covered in craft items and pushed against the walls, so he figured it was an oversize room for making Amish crafts.

When the room thinned out, he placed his music sheets on the pile. But several of the girls stayed to talk with Ivy. He still hadn't seen Holly. Maybe Ivy knew where she was, but Ivy was still talking with a few of the choir members. When she finished her conversation and waved goodbye to them, Joshua approached her.

"Hey, Josh. Denki for coming."

"No problem. It was fun." As much as he loved all things related to music, he didn't have many opportunities to enjoy the medium. "But . . .

I'm really only here because Holly invited me." He looked across the room once more. "Where did your sister disappear to?"

Displeasure seemed to fill Ivy's eyes. "Ya, about that." She sighed and held up a lyric sheet. "Apparently she passed this to one of the singers next to her, and that person passed it to me a few minutes ago when everyone was turning in their lyric sheets." Ivy gave the paper to him. There was a note written on the back: "I'm really tired, and I've got work early tomorrow. Josh is a great guy, and I know he won't mind taking you home after practice. ☺ —Holly"

"I saw her leaving and tried to mouth for her to stay, but I didn't want to interrupt our rehearsal by drawing attention to sibling stuff. Because if she was doing what I thought, we would've argued right then and there." Ivy rolled her eyes. "I'm sure you realize what is going on here every bit as much as I do."

Oh. Joshua felt his cheeks burn. Holly hadn't invited him to caroling practice so she could spend time with him outside of work-related tasks. She was passing him off to her sister.

Ivy's face mirrored his embarrassment. "Don't worry. When I get home, I'll let her have it. I should've suspected something earlier when she kept going on and on about you and how I would like you and how you love music and I love singing. I'm sorry."

Joshua stared at the ground. "It's not your fault. I'll drive you home." He drew a deep breath and squared his shoulders. "Unless . . . Would you rather I drop you off at the youth singing?"

"Nee, but denki. Normally I do attend, but Mamm and I have a house cleaning scheduled at six tomorrow morning, and if I went to the singing, I wouldn't be home until late." She tapped her papers against the crate, stacking them neatly before she tucked the pile under her arm. "Shall we?"

They walked outside and toward Joshua's waiting horse and rig. The other carolers had hurried off to get to the last of the games before the singing began.

"Ach. Just now thought of this, but"—Ivy opened the door to the carriage—"how do you have a horse and buggy here since you live so far away?"

Joshua held the door while she got in. He had intended to open it for her, but she beat him to it. "I had a driver drop me off at a cousin's place. Still in the next district over but not too far from here. The horse and rig belong to him."

Ivy's eyes met his, and the look on her face said she understood exactly what he'd done and why. He closed the door and walked around to his side.

Rather than having the driver drop him off here, he'd borrowed a horse and rig, thinking he was going to have the privilege of driving Holly home or maybe riding around with her for a while, getting time alone. How stupid could he be?

He grabbed the reins and released the brake. *Apparently very stupid.* They pulled out of the gravel driveway, and Ivy directed him toward her house.

"I'm sorry about my sister." Ivy stared at her folded hands that rested on the papers in her lap. "She can be . . . weird about these things. I was really hopeful when she met you that she might get over her aversion to socializing. I just want her to be happy, you know?"

"I'd like to speak with her when we get back to your house. I feel dumb about showing up. I'm sure I was the oldest one there, and I'm not normally a member of your youth singing group, so I stuck out like a sore thumb."

"No one thought anything about that, I'm sure. And you sounded great. You added a strong voice to our men's section. I hope you'll still join us for the caroling, despite my sister and her shady intentions."

It wasn't Ivy's fault, and he actually did enjoy the practice. What difference did it make if he was the oldest one and stuck out? He wanted to be a part of any music he could be. "Yeah, I can do that."

"Really?" She turned to face him. "I'm surprised but so glad."

He simply nodded, and they rode the rest of the way in silence.

Joshua pulled the rig up to the turnaround near the front porch. "Tell Holly I want to take a short ride with her. I won't keep her from her needed sleep."

Ivy nodded. "Of course. Denki, Josh. I'll see you next week." She hopped out of the buggy and entered the house.

When Holly finally heard carriage wheels grinding on the gravel driveway, she went to the front door and peered out the glass inlay. Dusk made the view rather gray, but streaks of gold and pink filled the sky. The horse and buggy Josh drove came to a halt on the driveway. Her plan of slipping out of practice was a good one. Their arriving this late had to mean they'd been riding around talking, right? He would most likely take to Ivy, and Ivy to him. Then he could have someone who wanted to find the right man and marry. Holly could then be guilt-free as she stayed focused on her mission to bring medicine to her community. If the plan was so good, why did she feel unhappy seeing her sister exit the carriage?

Ivy hurried up the steps and toward the door. Holly dashed to the nearby kitchen and pretended to be cleaning a dish as she heard the door open and close.

"Glad to see my dear, exhausted sister is resting in bed." Ivy leaned against the kitchen counter and crossed her arms as she glared at Holly.

"It wasn't a complete white lie. I am tired." Holly lowered her eyes back to the dishes. "And it was for the greater good of two people I care about."

"Look, I don't know who you think you're lying to, but I'm your sister. I was there when you met Josh, and I listened when you spent hours justifying to yourself why you needed to turn down dating him. You like him. I know it. You know it. Poor Josh is the only one confused by what's going on here. You should tell him how you feel. Both of you deserve some real honesty about now."

"I did tell him the very first day we reconnected. He was gleaning corn, and I stopped to talk with him. I told him that my work is too important to give up for a relationship."

Ivy rolled her eyes and huffed. "I'm going to bypass every silly thing you just said and stay focused on the only thing that matters right now. You told him that nearly a month ago, and since then you have called him, had dinner at his house, and gone on outings looking for Sam Miller in your Sunday best, and then *you* invited *him* to tonight's event."

"Ivy . . ."

"Oh, and he's waiting for you in his buggy."

"What?" Holly looked up, startled.

"He wants to talk to you."

This wasn't how she expected tonight to go. "Fine." She set the dish in the sink, dried her hands, and grabbed a sweater from the rack beside the front door. Once on the porch, she stood there, putting on her sweater and trying to find the courage to tell him the truth. During her year of knowing him—whether at a function for singles, dealing with Lyle's health emergency, or trying to find Sam Miller—they'd been good together. She liked the guy. A lot. How could she not? But that wasn't the point. If she married, the church leaders wouldn't allow her to continue her education or work at the pharmacy. And if she couldn't marry, then she shouldn't waste his time, no matter how much she liked being around him. She drew a deep breath and went down the stairs.

Josh nodded at her when she came in view. He wasn't smiling. He leaned across the seat and pushed her door open. "Get in. We won't talk long."

Her heart pounded as she wordlessly complied. The horse clippety-clopped, and the buggy ambled as Josh pulled onto the road.

After a few moments of riding in silence, she felt compelled to speak up. "Are you mad at me?" The answer was rather obvious, but she hoped it would cause him to say something. She looked over at him, but he kept his eyes on the road.

"A bit." Another moment of silence passed. "Look, Holly, I knew up front that you weren't interested in a relationship, for whatever reason. But I really feel duped here. You invited me to go to a fun event outside of our task of finding Sam Miller. What was I supposed to think? Your sister is nice and all, but she's not you. She's not the person I've been unable to get off my mind for months, despite my best efforts. She's not the person I've been able to laugh with effortlessly. And she's not the only woman I have ever felt some unexplainable connection with. I wouldn't say any of that except I think you feel something for me too. Is that all in my head?"

Guilt tried to suffocate her. While she kept her heart hidden away, he was raw and vulnerable. Who stayed this calm when angry? Who was this honest about how they felt? Certainly not her. But his honesty had backed her into a corner, and she didn't know how to get out of it without hurting him more.

"No." The word was barely audible. She cleared her throat. "No, it's not all in your head. But I . . . I just can't. I know that, so I wanted to discourage you from thinking what we feel could lead to more. I wanted to spare you heartache."

"First, it's not your job to spare me heartache. Why can't you at least give us a shot before you decide *you can't*? Whatever that means."

Emotions bubbled in her as if she had a teakettle boiling in her chest, creating a pressure that was ready to screech and release steam. "Because I could never be a good wife to you!" She sat there breathless, unable to believe what she'd let escape from her mouth.

He stared at her. "I'm not talking about marriage, Holly. I just want to see you and get to know you better." Josh's voice remained quiet and even-keeled despite her frantic reaction. She hadn't meant to raise her voice.

"But that's always the goal." She folded her arms across her waist, squeezing tight, trying to keep control of her voice. "That's the goal of the singings and every other type of social event—to find a suitable spouse. I'll never be a suitable spouse for an Amish man."

"Because you work?"

Holly nodded as a few tears escaped. She hadn't expected him to unearth such feelings, feelings that went deeper than she had realized.

"Holly, I don't want to change you. I only want to spend time with you. And I would never ask you to give up your work at the pharmacy."

Holly shook her head. "Come on, Josh. You were raised just like me. A young married Amish woman can't work outside the home, not those first few years. If money is too tight, the ministers will allow her to clean an Englisch home one day a week or take her babies in tow while she sells produce or baked goods. She certainly would not be allowed to hold a job with set hours, and Amish tradition aside, children deserve a mother who could care for them full time. The older women judge and critique how well the younger women are tending to their husbands, and if any woman isn't handling the home well, there's trouble—lots of it."

He studied her. "It's not . . ."

Was he going to dispute that the situation for young married women was that bad? If so, he'd apparently changed his mind. Older married women, especially those with their youngest child in school or those past childbearing years, had more wiggle room. But she couldn't afford to lose momentum for her people by taking a sabbatical for the next fifteen to twenty years. She and Josh were caught, and there wasn't a solution.

But maybe now he understood.

She stared straight ahead, wishing things were different. "There's really nothing else to say, Josh. I'm not the kind of person who could give up everything to tend to her husband and babies. Would you want to give up who you are, give up running Smucker Farms, to marry me? There are young Amish women who are praying to find someone like you, women who long to stop working outside the home and have babies."

She looked out the window, hoping he didn't see her tears in the dim lighting. "Please take me home. I understand if you can't help me anymore. You have certainly done a lot."

Josh sighed, but he didn't say anything else.

When she joined the church at seventeen, she knew she was signing up for a life of celibacy. It hadn't mattered to her then, but she hadn't known someone like Josh would come along. Still, she couldn't stop following what God had put inside her before she met Josh.

But her heart was breaking.

19

*B*randon added another name to the list of patients who needed to be more consistent in picking up their medications. If he could get them to be more compliant in taking their meds as their doctors prescribed, Greene's star rating would go up a little. He noticed someone walking close to the counter next to his workstation.

"Hello, I will be right with you. Just give me one second." Thankfully this Tuesday morning had been pretty slow customerwise. He clicked the button to finish the list and make the computer send an alert when one of these patients' profiles was accessed. "Dropping off or picking up?" he asked without looking away from the screen.

"Well, I was intending to drop off this food. But if you want me to pick you up and make you eat it, I could."

Jules. He grinned at her and leaned over the counter, looking at her petite frame. She was holding the leash of a yellow Lab that was wearing a blue therapy vest. The animal was sitting still at her feet. "You sure? I'm pretty certain I outweigh you by a lot. And your beast doesn't look very ferocious."

"I once caught a former linebacker when he fainted during a blood draw, and I managed to get him safely in a chair, so I think I could handle you."

"How on earth did you do that?"

She laughed. "I have no idea. I actually have no idea how we manage lots of things we need to do to provide health care to Raysburg, but we do it."

"Yeah, you do." He returned her smile. "What's with the dog? Tell me that my dad isn't allowing dogs to pick up their own prescriptions now." He was teasing, but they did fill scripts for dogs.

Julie scratched the yellow dog between his ears. "His name is Nacho. He's my pet, but he's also a therapy dog, which is why he's allowed in stores. I find that his presence helps many children relax when they're stressed, especially Amish children. But right now he's off duty."

The animal, that by Brandon's best guess had to weigh more than a hundred pounds, blinked serenely and opened his mouth to pant.

Julie waggled the large bag. "Hungry?"

Besides his own parents, he couldn't think of anyone who had brought him food, and she did it in the middle of her own busy workday. "It looks as if you have more than one to-go order."

"I do. I was going to drop your lunch off if you were busy, but if not . . ."

Brandon tried to wipe the smile off his face, but the idea of good conversation over lunch really made his day. Something uncomfortable nagged at him, and a moment later he realized what it was. *Mila.* Jules didn't know he had a girlfriend. He wasn't keeping it a secret. It just hadn't come up. Should he tell her? Seemed to him that he and Jules were simply colleagues of sorts, and if he mentioned Mila now, he'd make Jules uncomfortable for absolutely no reason. "So where would you like to go eat?"

"I know it's mid-November, but it's still decently warm in the sun at this hour of the day. Maybe have an alfresco lunch? There are some benches on the square."

"That sounds nice." It actually sounded wonderful.

A few minutes later they were sitting on the bench, Nacho was comfortably settled in the grass, and Brandon was relishing being off his feet and sitting in the sunshine. It had to be in the midfifties, definitely chilly to be sitting, but the warm sun on his face felt nice, and the hot sandwich from the diner hit the spot.

"This is really tasty. I don't think I would have thought to order something called a meatloaf sandwich, but it's a lot better than it sounds." Brandon wiped his mouth and looked over to Julie's side of the bench. She was only halfway through her sandwich.

She took a swig of her soda from its glass bottle. "You may be used to fancier lunch options in the city, but there are perks to living out here too, number one being the people."

"You know, I grew up pretty close to Raysburg, but I never felt like a real part of this town. Probably because I was always plotting my escape." Brandon crumbled the now-empty sandwich paper and placed it in the paper bag.

She dabbed her lips with a napkin. "As hard as it may be for you to believe, I moved here by choice. And I love it. I might have been able to achieve more prestige working in a rich part of Philly or even the nearby suburbs, but my patients here are the salt of the earth."

Her description stirred something inside him. His goal for so long had been to earn his degree and make all the money he could. When was the last time he really considered *who* he filled the meds for? Working in his dad's pharmacy these few weeks, he'd met all kinds of people. Amish men and women who often didn't have a clue how the medications worked but were still so grateful to have them. Elderly retirees on fixed incomes who seemed happy to have an old-timey pharmacy that still operated the way pharmacies did during their youth. And young adult patients who weren't jaded like he was about small-town living.

"Yeah, I guess 'salt of the earth' is a good term for them. I'm really hoping to implement some ideas to make my dad's store more profitable. The town needs him."

Jules nodded. "We do need him. And he needs you."

He hadn't expected it to feel good to be needed. Not a dime-a-dozen pharmacist floating from store to store for a big-box company, one in a sea of others. Did he really want to spend his life doling out medications to strangers he had no connection to and who cared nothing about him?

"So you mentioned you could have worked in Philly and something about prestige? Where exactly are you from, Jules?" He hoped to lighten the mood from the heavier topics his brain had been dwelling on.

"That is a conversation for another day, Brandon Greene." She balled up the empty paper that had once held her sandwich and placed it in the paper bag along with Brandon's trash. "You'll have to stick around to find out." She rose from the bench, and Nacho got up too. "Not that I would try to bribe you to stick around with cheap lunches and boring stories of my life." She rolled her eyes and laughed before she tossed their empty lunch bag into a nearby garbage can. "Unless you think that would do the trick."

He laughed and followed her. There was no denying they had something going on between them, even if Brandon couldn't be sure as to what. It was a spark that was easygoing, something he didn't have with Mila. Nothing came easy with Mila. He always felt as if he had to work for her affection and approval. He'd stayed committed to the relationship out of hope they would get to a place of enjoying life after he graduated and was working. There was nothing wrong with hoping to be in a better place, except they should be savoring where they were now, right? They were young and had good lives, and yet happiness always seemed just out of reach. Would it still be out of reach ten years from now? The answer that came to him cut deep. He sighed as he realized he needed to make a difficult phone call that was long overdue.

"Hey, Jules." They stopped on the corner of Main and Hopper. "I'm not ready to head back to work yet. You go on, and I'll catch up with you another time. Thanks for lunch."

"No problem. Bye, Brandon." She waved as she walked toward the clinic, her yellow Lab at her side.

Brandon stood, pulled his cell out of his pocket, and stared at Mila's number on the Favorites screen. He and Julie might never go on a date or be anything more than friends, but that didn't change the fact that he and Mila weren't going to work out. He might not be as altruistic as Julie, his dad, or Holly, but his and Mila's goals and values were too far apart, and the gulf was only widening. He had to break things off with her.

He didn't want to do it by text, but he also didn't want to blindside her by calling. His fingers flew across the screen as he composed a text.

> We need to have a hard conversation.
> Can we speak on the phone?

> K.

Although he'd warned her he was calling, the phone rang three times before she answered.

"What's this about? You going to tell me you're moving to the boonies for good?"

Best to cut straight to the chase. Rip off the Band-Aid. "Mila, I don't think we should see each other anymore."

"What? *Why?*" Her voice rose half an octave on the second word.

"It's just that this time apart . . . has made it clear that we aren't as good together as I thought we were."

"Wait, wait, wait. *You're* breaking up with *me?*" She was almost yelling by the end of the question.

What does that mean? "Is this a big shock? We haven't been connecting for months, even before I left for Raysburg."

"You don't understand." She made a sound that signaled frustration. "I've been the patient one."

"Patient?"

"Yeah, patient. You never have money or time for us to enjoy life, but I knew you'd have both within a few months. And you seemed to be a good friend. You actually care about others, unlike most people I know. But apparently not about me. Now I've wasted so much time waiting, and for what? To be dumped right before you get your license?"

Brandon recoiled from the phone. He didn't expect her reaction to be happy, but this wasn't what he expected. "I wasn't thinking of it that way. I'm sorry. I never asked you to waste your time. But maybe if we were good together, you wouldn't think of it as a waste."

"You really don't get it."

Was their entire relationship some sort of exercise in patience for her rather than the partnership he'd thought they had? "Can you help me understand?"

"Seriously? If I have to explain further, then there's no hope. I guess you made the right call."

They were both quiet for a moment, the silence weighing as heavy as the thick snow that would soon blanket their state. He couldn't even ask to retain her friendship after a conversation like this. Not right now.

"Mila—"

"There's really nothing more to say. Goodbye, Brandon. I would tell you, 'I hope you enjoy your life,' but I really don't mean that right now."

"Fair enough." The phone beeped as she hung up on him.

Brandon took a deep breath, running his hand through his short hair. He sank back down on the bench. Breaking up was the right thing to do, even though it currently felt horrible.

From: store7006@bbdrugs.com
To: mikeprice@bbdrugs.com
Subject: re: Possible Acquisition
November 14, 2017

It seems that Lyle Greene is still in a bind with the pending charges he will face from the PA State Board of Pharmacy, and perhaps that'll be the push he needs to sell. As soon as the December board meeting is over, we should move to make him an offer. Depending on the consequences he faces, he might owe a decent amount of money. Besides, the deal we can make him will give him some funds to put down for retirement. It will be the best option for him, and he will have to take it.

20

*S*tanding on a stepladder inside the storefront window, Holly tapped another tiny nail into the soft wood. There was plenty of room at the front of Greene's to decorate. It was a corner store with beautiful bay windows facing each street. Ivy followed her on a separate ladder hanging tinsel and a garland. Since the store was decorated each year, it seemed that it would at least have the nails in the right place for hanging trimmings, but that was never the case, because Ivy changed the displays every year.

Her sister hummed "Deck the Halls."

Holly would love to feel one smidgen as happy about life as Ivy did. If the whole issue of liking Josh wasn't painful enough, she ached with embarrassment for trying to sneakily set him up with Ivy. Why would she think doing something like that was okay? How had she fooled herself into believing she wouldn't mind if Josh liked Ivy more than her?

What had started as Ivy quietly humming had now progressed to singing, and she wasn't being all that reserved about it.

"Must you?" Holly really needed some peace and quiet. Her misery seemed to need unhindered time to contemplate.

"Yes, I must," Ivy managed to reply to Holly between verses and didn't miss a beat of the song. No one loved Christmas the way Ivy did.

Each year since Lyle's wife, Beverly, died, Ivy was responsible for decorating the store for holidays. Ivy and Holly had arrived at Greene's two hours before its ten o'clock opening, and it was now approaching ten. Surely Ivy was almost finished, although there were two more large and suspicious boxes that she had pulled from storage. Holly had no clue of their contents.

"Are we about done here?" She needed to get in her rig soon and head for the Miller family reunion. Hopefully, Sam Miller would be there.

"Done? Ha. All we've put up is one animatronic snowman, a puffy snow scene in the window, jingle bells around the door, and this tinsel stuff."

"And the Christmas tree."

"*And* the Christmas tree," Ivy agreed. "Too bad we can't have one in our home. Although I suppose it makes it more special for us and other Amish to visit here."

Holly glanced at the tree in question. It was a live Canaan fir, grown at a local Christmas tree farm, and they had decorated it with beautiful handmade ornaments, most of them gifts from Lyle's patients over the years. It had already given the pharmacy a wonderful piney smell, which mingled with the cinnamon scent from the straw broom Ivy had placed in the snowman's stick hands.

"You aren't the first Amish kid to want a tree in the house, but I think it's nice not to have distractions in our home—just a focus on Christ's birth. But I do love your annual Christmas window here at Greene's."

"I hope you find your patient today." After securing the ends of the garland, Ivy climbed down and folded her ladder.

"I really hope so too. It'll be a little awkward showing up at a family reunion that isn't my family." Holly stepped off her ladder and moved it and Ivy's aside to be put in the storage room later.

"Wasn't Josh going with you?"

"That was our original plan before I played matchmaker."

"Ya, *that* was a brilliant plan. But I was pleasantly surprised when he agreed to participate in the Christmas caroling without you. I think he just likes music. And he wanted to follow through with the commitment. Look how much he has already put into helping you find this Sam Miller. He's a good one, Holly."

"He is." Holly looked at the ground. She'd known that about Josh not long after meeting him. He was a great guy, but that didn't change that she wasn't available. Keys jingled as the back door opened, and Holly knew Todd had arrived. He would go to his station to start filling scripts without interrupting them.

Ivy tucked the remaining tinsel inside its box. "What gave you that crazy idea to attempt to romantically set up him and me? A blind man could see that you are the one he likes."

"Look, Ivy, you know what's going on here." Holly spoke quietly, hoping Todd didn't overhear them. "I can never marry, so why waste his time dating?"

Ivy put a hand on Holly's arm and waited until their eyes met. "You know that Daed wouldn't want you to give up your life, right? You don't have to give up your own happiness in order to help our people get medicine. Besides, as much as I believe in your cause, you have to accept that with or without you enlightening and prodding them, people have a responsibility to pay attention to the pain in their bodies, listen to the doctor, and take the medicine prescribed. Our people need what you're doing. We do. But you can't take so much responsibility to get the message out that you sacrifice your whole life."

Holly rearranged a nativity set in the bay window. "But you know what would be expected of me if I were to marry. The Amish expect marriage and children to take up a woman's whole life."

Ivy shrugged. "The Amish as a whole didn't approve of you becoming a GED-educated pharmacy tech either, but you are one, *and* you have our bishop's approval. And now you're studying for the entrance exam to nursing school. When you get in, you'll earn your LPN degree—with his blessing."

"Ya." Holly held the small manger, cleaning dust off baby Jesus's face. "But when the bishop agreed to my getting my GED and going to nursing school if I could pass the exam, he was very clear about his expectations and my future." Holly set the manger back in place.

"Our bishop is a good man, and good men listen to reason and change their stance. He won't change it today, and maybe not even in a year. But I believe you can win him over. So tell me again, who says you and Josh can't live your lives in your own way? A way that both respects our Amish faith and allows you to follow your God-given mission."

"It's not—" Holly shook her head. "It's not that easy."

"Of course it won't be easy. All valuable things take work, like your GED and convincing the Amish of the importance of medicine. If anyone knows how to focus on what has value and to be patient with the Amish ways while working with and around them, it's you. And that's all I've got." Ivy hugged her.

Holly closed her eyes as they embraced. Was Ivy right? Her sister had planted hope, but even so, Holly knew Amish tradition wasn't the only brick wall that stood firm. Still . . . "How did you get to be so smart?"

Ivy squeezed her tight. "By taking lessons from you."

As Holly pulled away, she looked up and noticed the time on the wall clock. "Oh, rats! It's already three minutes after ten o'clock, and I haven't unlocked the doors."

"You better get to the reunion." Ivy grabbed Holly's coat off a box. "I'll remind Todd you're off this morning. Come by the store and see my finished creation later." Ivy winked at her.

Holly took her coat. She flipped the sign on the door so Open was facing out and then fiddled with the old lock. It clicked, and she exited the store. The mid-November wind sent a chill through her, and she put on her coat and looked around her side in search of the belt to tie it.

"Oof." She had run into something—or rather someone, tall and warm.

Strong hands steadied her as she looked up into the brown eyes of Josh. What was he doing here? His smile was faint, but she supposed any smile was a good sign.

"I thought you didn't run late?"

She backed up, totally unprepared to see him. "Only when you show up apparently." Was Ivy truly correct? Would a life with him be possible? Would he even be interested after all she'd put him through?

"I looked in the store window, and since you seemed to be finishing some major decorating project, I was waiting out here. Ready to go to the Millers' anniversary party?"

"Go to the . . ." Who was this true to their word? "You . . . don't mind going with me? Even after what happened Sunday?"

He stared at her. "I told you I'd help, and I'm going to follow through."

A cold shiver of guilt ran through her while embarrassment burned the back of her neck and cheeks. "I'm sorry, Josh. I really am. It was foolish and pushy to try to set you up with Ivy."

"Apology accepted." His warm eyes seemed to embrace her—the parts of her he understood as well as the ones he didn't. "Other than inviting me to go to the caroling practice Sunday, you've been very up-front in your stance about not dating. I've decided I'm fine respecting that and just being a friend."

His casual mannerisms seemed to confirm that he'd reevaluated her and dating her was no longer on his list. That was a good thing. So why did it hurt?

"Josh." She paused, unsure if she should say the rest of the sentence. "If I were ever willing to date or marry, you would be the reason."

He angled his head, looking taken aback. A few moments later he smiled. "I'm willing to be comfortable with that if you are."

Wow. How was it possible she'd found someone so open and agreeable? "I am."

He smiled. "About time you were agreeable to something." He gestured toward a car. "It's a long way to the Miller party by horse and carriage. My plan is better. Okay?"

When the driver stopped the car in the driveway of the Miller anniversary party, Joshua got out of the back seat. Holly slid across the seat and followed him. The place was a sea of tethered horses and parked buggies. All these rigs for one couple's seventy-fifth anniversary? But if his own parents had a gathering like this one day, he suspected it would be the same.

"You wanted Millers. I found you some Millers." Joshua gestured at the large number of rigs.

Holly smiled. "I actually just need a particular one if you can work that miracle."

"That I'm still working on."

It was good they could still laugh together. He'd been so angry after she left the singing Sunday evening. A week of working with his chickens had lessened his temper but not his disappointment. Still, even time with Holly as friends was better than no time at all.

They walked into a large building that Joshua knew was used for timber framing. Lots of men, most bearing some similar familial features, were chatting quietly, while women were setting the large table for a meal. Children were helping their mothers with the table, and a few were gathered around the elderly couple seated at the head of the table. That had to be Noah and Rachel.

"Good morning." He paused near one of the groups closest to him. "I'm Joshua Smucker, and this is Holly Zook."

The three men and two women greeted them warmly and soon were talking with them about chicken farming and Joshua's and Holly's relatives that they knew. Joshua let the chatter go on for a bit before he shifted the focus. "The reason we're here is I spoke to Simon Miller at a fall festival last week, and he invited me to come here because we're trying to find a Sam Miller. My friend Holly needs to talk to him."

One of the older men wearing a hat gave a short laugh. "My name is Sam Miller."

Joshua glanced at Holly. She shook her head, indicating this wasn't the man she had seen on the tape.

"Good to meet you." Joshua shook his hand. "But we're looking for a Sam Miller who went to Greene's Pharmacy in Raysburg in October."

One of the men near Joshua called out to another man. "Hey, Sam. You been to Greene's Pharmacy lately?"

The man shook his head. "Nee."

A few more men came to see what the conversation was about. Joshua explained the situation again.

"Excuse me. I may be able to help you." A middle-aged man stepped around his family members to stand in front of Joshua and Holly. "You said Sam Miller who went to a pharmacy in Raysburg?"

"Ya," Holly confirmed. Joshua could hear the excitement rising in her voice.

"My cousin Sam Miller and I were in Raysburg back in October, the weekend of the fourteenth and fifteenth."

"Is he here today?" Joshua asked. Maybe, just maybe, they could catch a break.

"Afraid not. He sent his regards to Noah and Rachel, but he's working today, trying to catch up with all the orders before their shop closes for Thanksgiving. Sometimes I contract to work with him when he gets too busy. Come to think of it, he did mention needing to go to a pharmacy while we were there. He needed to get some medicine. Something about his heart, and it couldn't wait."

Holly was grinning as if they had won a prize. "That must be him! Can you give us his cell phone number?"

The man's eyes widened. "He has a new cell number, and all I have is his old number. He'd had his former number a long time, but for some reason about six weeks back, he started getting a bazillion weird calls a day. He said it was as if someone used his number to start an illicit business or something. I can give you the old number I have for him."

"I have the old one, but denki." Holly shifted her weight from one foot to another. This had to be frustrating for her to get so close to having the man's number but it to remain just out of reach. "What you said could explain why we haven't been able to reach him by the number he had on file. What about a current address?"

"'Fraid he has a few addresses he stays at."

"A few?" Holly's voice rose in pitch.

"He's single and works at several locations. He usually stays with Amish friends and family when on the road. He's a certified housing inspector for new construction. He's one of the few Amish who can do that job because he studied electric wiring. You know what? I've got his boss's phone number and an address where he'll be working the week after Thanksgiving. But it's a pretty long ways from here. You got a pen?"

"Ya, I do." Joshua pulled it from his pocket along with his pad of paper. "Go ahead."

After the man gave him the address, Joshua reached out to shake his hand. "Denki, this is very helpful."

"Thank you. Thank you so much." Holly's blue eyes were sparkling.

Joshua smiled, but he felt torn. He was thrilled for her breakthrough. But that also meant the time was coming soon when he wouldn't have an excuse to see her.

He really was his own worst enemy.

21

*V*oices from outside the tiny office space in the storage room were dull and soft, and Brandon found them easy to tune out. Six days ago Holly was given an address that should lead to the right Sam Miller, but only time would tell. Brandon tapped his fingers impatiently on his laptop as he waited for the high-definition videos to download from the flash drive. He glanced at the closed door and wondered if he should have invited his dad or Holly to see this new security footage. But Dad felt so guilty about his memory problems, and Brandon didn't want to remind him by showing footage of the day he lost unless Brandon discovered a real lead.

About an hour ago Brandon had signed for a confidential package from MediSecure, a remote security company. He'd wanted to open the package right then, but he'd steadied his emotions and completed his normal pharmacy tasks. Then he had ducked into this private room so he could watch the footage away from everyone else.

After what felt like hours, the videos finished saving to his computer. He opened the file from Sunday, October fifteenth, and hit Play and then went to double speed to watch it faster. When the one Amish customer of the day came into view, Brandon paused the video. The view was from a different angle than they'd previously seen, but it didn't tell him anything more than what they already knew about Sam Miller.

He hit Play again and watched his dad use the computer to make labels for the bottles, hit Print, and then fill the five medications. His dad wrote a note and placed it on his to-do pile. Brandon hit Pause. His heart thudded. There *was* a note after all. Why had none of their many thorough searches uncovered it? He backed up the footage and zoomed in, feeling his temples pulse.

Even with the high-definition footage zoomed in, he wasn't able to decipher the note, but maybe if he focused on the to-do pile, he could figure out what happened to it. He hit fast-forward, watching his dad close the pharmacy and turn off the lights. Brandon opened the file for Monday and kept it in fast-forward mode, watching the pile of notes. He saw Holly shuffle through the notes, show one to Lyle, and put it back. She then took her delivery items and left.

As Brandon watched his dad fall, his heart dropped, his face grew hot, and tears brimmed. Despite everything that had happened in their adult lives, he loved that man. In the hustle and stress of school and bills, he'd forgotten just how much he loved him, but it was more than he could ever say. What would've happened if Dad had died before the two of them had resolved things? Being forced to stay in Raysburg had been a blessing, not an inconvenience or a curse.

He could only see his dad's feet as the footage showed Holly discovering his dad. A few stray tears rolled down his cheeks as he watched her panicked movements, clearly responding as a woman who loved his dad. The Amish guy who'd entered the pharmacy with her—Josh something— seemed to calm her. Then the EMTs came in and removed Dad from the pharmacy. Nothing else happened for a while. Hours later Adrienne came in, working hard to catch up. Holly returned later in the day, quickly trying to get all things pharmacy related back on track. They added a few more notes to the pile but didn't remove any.

The footage showed nothing different concerning the to-do stack in the following few days. He saw himself as well as Holly, Adrienne, and Harris talking with patients and filling medications. He opened the file of Saturday, October 21. This was the day of the health fair and Todd's first day. He arrived early and stayed focused. Brandon saw him clicking on the computer for a while before turning his attention to the pile of papers and flipping through them. Since Brandon was searching for what happened to his dad's note, he slowed the video to normal speed. Maybe Todd had dropped it while looking at messages and dealing with customers' insurance companies.

After several minutes of video, it appeared that Todd had found the paper his dad had written. Even though Brandon couldn't read it, he recognized the note by the pattern of words. Under the note he could see what seemed to be labels removed from prescription bottles. At last a clue! Todd read the note carefully. He stood with it in his hand, as if reading it several times, before he flipped through the labels and then turned around and shredded all of it.

Wait! Brandon gasped and clicked to watch it again. He leaned in as if he were half-blind and hit Play. He couldn't believe his own eyes. *Why?* What reason would Todd have for destroying what his dad had written about the patient? And the labels? If the scripts were missing information in the computer, the labels held the missing pieces. An even bigger question was, Why hadn't Todd mentioned the incident when he knew they were scouring every nook and cranny for it?

Sweat beaded across Brandon's forehead as his heart raced. He watched as Todd walked outside the camera's scope. Then he came back into view and shredded several other documents. *This can't be happening.* Brandon couldn't move as his brain tried to reject this reality.

But it did happen, and Brandon bet the footage was showing Todd shredding the records Lyle created the day Sam Miller came into the pharmacy, the paperwork that should've been Greene's hard copies. "That lying, deceitful . . ."

Memories of his dad's hesitation to hire Todd pressed in, refusing to be ignored. What exactly had happened between the two men all those years ago? Was it enough to cause Todd to sabotage the pharmacy? And why had Brandon been so arrogant to think he knew better than his dad?

He had no answers to those questions or any answers to the question of what to do next.

He got up, opened the door, and peered into the pharmacy. Holly was at the counter counting pills. He stuck his head out. "Holly?"

She finished counting and looked up. "Yes?"

"Could you join me for just a minute? It won't take long."

"Sure." She finished what she was doing and then walked toward him. Brandon held open the door, and once she was in the small room, he shut it behind her.

He drew a breath, determined to speak low and even. "I need your assurance that what I'm about to tell you won't leave this room. Not yet anyway."

Holly's eyes opened wide. "What's going on?"

"I found out what happened to the scripts. I even have video evidence." He leaned down to his laptop, pulled up that particular Saturday's video, and rewound to the spot where Todd shredded the note and the five labels.

She leaned in closer to the screen. "What's he doing?"

"That's the note Dad created on Sunday, October fifteenth. I bet it had vital information about the prescriptions and where they are from.

And those appear to be labels from empty prescription bottles. I bet they're for our five missing heart med scripts. Todd is shredding them. Now watch." He hit fast-forward to the part where Todd returned from a different area and shredded a few more pieces of paper. "Based on their color and size, I'm willing to wager those are the printed hard copies that Dad made. And it's a safe bet that after he did this, he went into the prescription editor on the computer and removed information like the doctor's name, practice, and NPI number."

"So you're saying . . ."

"I'm saying this evidence shows that Todd deliberately sabotaged us. And if he was willing to do this, I feel certain he reported to the board that we were filling scripts without a doctor's prescription. I didn't ask any of the relief pharmacists if they filed a report because the innocent as well as the guilty would have given me the same answer: 'I didn't turn in anything to the board.' And like Dad said, it might have been that the board inspector uncovered the missing information while we weren't in the pharmacy."

"Wow." Holly plunked into the chair. Brandon took a few breaths in silence as he tried to adjust to the shock of Todd's betrayal. Holly's hands closed into fists, and moments later her knuckles were white. "What do we do now?" She looked up at Brandon. "Are we going upstairs to tell Lyle?"

"No, not yet. I don't want to cause him that kind of stress, and the best way to avoid that is to remain quiet until I have a solution. I want Dad well and with us for many years to come. The problem is we need Todd. I'm not licensed, and the other pharmacists can't work enough hours to make up for us not having Todd. We can't just close shop during Todd's usual hours until I get my license."

Holly glared at the door. "I wish we could confront him right now." She crossed her arms. "How can we let him continue working here? What if he does something else?"

Brandon shook his head. "I don't think he would. It wouldn't be likely for Greene's to suddenly start operating illegally after so many years of carefully following the law. The board would be suspicious of who was working here other than Dad and would start looking further into things. What Todd did was set us up for fines that would force Dad to sell the pharmacy and personally go bankrupt. He doesn't have to do anything else now but sit and wait. However, just in case, you and I are going to keep our eyes on him one hundred percent of the time he is in the building, starting right now."

Holly nodded. "Okay."

"He's not working tomorrow. Adrienne will be here, and I'll be taking my licensing exams."

"Tomorrow? Oh, Brandon, I didn't realize they were coming up so soon. Are you ready?"

"I sure hope I am. I can't say I feel ready. But I'm not sure I ever would." If he came this far and failed one or both of them . . . He shuddered at the thought.

22

*H*olly looked out the back passenger window as the sedan slowed and turned into the unfinished subdivision. Josh was across from her, lightly tapping on the armrest.

Of all the places she could imagine finding their missing patient, this would never have entered her mind.

"Looks like this is the place." Josh gave Holly a half smile as their driver pulled up to the run-down trailer that was supposed to be the workplace of Sam Miller.

"Please, please, let this be the right person," Holly prayed aloud. Maybe, just maybe, this would be the break they needed. The sting of betrayal from Todd had stolen most of her sleep lately. How could anyone purposely try to ruin the life of someone as kind as Lyle? And take advantage of the man as he recuperated from the stroke? That was really low. She had kept her promise to Brandon and not spoken of Todd's actions, not to anyone, not even to Josh. They needed this to be the right Sam Miller. They needed this to work out.

Josh grabbed the door handle. "I really think we'll get to talk to the right man. But if by chance we still have the wrong Sam Miller, we will regroup and keep at it until we find the right one. Got it?"

It was suddenly easier to breathe. "Ya, I got it." Armed with his confidence, she opened her door.

Josh exited the vehicle too. Before he closed the door, he leaned in to speak to the driver. "We'll probably need thirty minutes or so if you want to run an errand or something."

"Sounds good. When I get back, I'll park around the side where there's shade." The driver nodded at both Josh and Holly.

"Good plan." Josh closed the door. He caught her looking his way, and he smiled.

Her face flushed with warmth. Why did he have to have such an effect on her?

When they were together, she felt like this daunting task—and many more—were possible. They *would* clear the pharmacy's name, and they could accomplish even more together through his connections in his community.

They walked to the front door of the trailer, and Josh knocked on the flimsy metal. The door opened after just a few seconds.

"Hello." A large Amish man greeted them. Holly could see that behind him were desks and lots of papers spread across them. He looked from Josh to Holly. "You two must be from Greene's Pharmacy."

"That's right." Josh smiled and held out his hand. The man shook it. "I'm Joshua Smucker, and this is Holly Zook."

"Hello." Holly also shook the man's hand. "I think we spoke on the phone. You are Elmer, right?"

He had been pleasant during their call and seemed glad to help. Hopefully the Sam Miller in his employ would be the one they were looking for. She hadn't even considered what would happen if they found the right man and for some reason he was uncooperative.

"Come on in. Welcome to our very, very humble abode." He stood to the side as they walked in. "Sorry about the mess. It's just the way temporary construction offices look." He held up one finger as he drew a two-way radio to his lips. "Sam, you there?"

The two-way crackled. "Here, boss."

"The people I mentioned earlier are here. Could you return to the office?"

"On my way."

He lowered the radio. "He'll be here shortly. One of the workers needed him to inspect something before he could continue with his job."

"Not a problem," Josh said.

Holly would have taken a seat, but the few chairs in the trailer were covered with folders. Papers were stacked on the desks and the floor, empty foam coffee cups were strewn about, and several large rulers and protractors were lying among the papers. Holly couldn't imagine working in a place like this. Not only was being tidy and well-organized her personal preference, but Lyle always emphasized that keeping the pharmacy clean and organized was essential.

"Our company is fairly large," Elmer said. "We're building homes all over the state, but we only have one Amish man who can inspect the electrical wiring, so Sam stays pretty busy and travels constantly."

Josh's eyes met Holly's, and he looked as hopeful as she felt. The trailer door swung open, and a man stepped inside. Could it actually be . . .

"Sam Miller?" Holly stepped toward him as he closed the door.

"That's me. What can I help you with?" The man smiled as he looked from Holly to Josh.

"I'm Holly Zook from Greene's Pharmacy in Raysburg. We're looking for a Sam Miller who went to the pharmacy on a Sunday in mid-October."

"That was me. Got several prescriptions filled." He tapped his chest. "I have heart issues, and I'd let myself run slap out of my medicines."

Josh thrust his hand forward. "We are very glad to finally meet you, Sam." He shook his hand, grinning. "Over the past few weeks we met a bunch of your relatives in the hope of having this conversation."

Sam laughed in a few short bursts. "Can't say people have wanted to meet me this badly before." He stroked his chin with its slightly gray stubble. "Did I shortchange the man somehow?"

"No, nothing like that." Relief swept through Holly, and it was all she could do to keep from hugging the man. She tried to keep herself professional, and it would help if she could stop grinning. "It's kind of a long story. I work at Greene's as a pharmacy tech."

"You, an Amish girl?" He looked to Josh, as if he needed a man to assure him it was okay for a woman to work there.

"Ya." Holly responded. "Strange, I know, but that pharmacy means a lot to the Amish, and the Amish mean a lot to me, so it all works out well, I think."

Josh nodded. "The bishop thinks it's a smart move for the community. Chances are you had heard about that pharmacy because of how hard Holly works to get the word out and how welcome the Amish feel at Greene's even on a Sunday or even if they don't have all the funds needed to pay for their medications."

The man's lips thinned. "Everything you said is true. I was there because I'd heard about it through the Amish grapevine. Just didn't expect an Amish girl to be behind all the buzz, that's all."

Holly tugged at the folds of her dress. "And yet here I am." She grinned. It didn't bother her that Amish men needed time to warm up to her less-than-typical life. "So . . . is it okay if we speak freely about your pharmacy visit in front of my friend Joshua and your boss?"

"Don't mind me." Elmer gathered some papers. "I'm on my way out anyway." He waved and exited the trailer.

"Sure," Sam agreed.

"You remember my boss, Lyle Greene? He filled your prescriptions."

"That's right. He was very helpful, which was good, because I needed those meds, and the pharmacy I use in Pottersville was closed."

So it *was* an emergency fill. Holly didn't know all the rules of pharmacy law in Pennsylvania, but she did know there were special allowances for emergency fills. "Lyle has had some medical troubles himself, and it affected his memory of that Sunday. Because of that and the fact that we need to prove to the Board of Pharmacy that your prescriptions are legitimate, our pharmacy is in a bit of trouble, and it would help us *very* much if we could get a statement from you about exactly what happened on that day."

"I'm sorry to hear about Lyle. Such a nice fella. I'll pray for his health, and I would be glad to help in any way I can."

Holly spent the next few minutes collecting the bits of vital information they were missing. Sam Miller's date of birth and his correct phone number. The physician's info: the doctor's name, which was Christine Smith, the name of her practice, the address, and the phone number. And all the identifying information of the original pharmacy from which the medications were supposed to be transferred. With each bit he shared, joy filled her. It felt the same as when she gathered around a table with her family completing a jigsaw puzzle and she was the lucky one to find all the key pieces, turning a jumbled mess into a clear picture.

"I know life is busy and I'm asking a lot, but do you think you could send a signed, notarized statement about what happened on Sunday, October fifteenth, to the pharmacy?"

"Sure. I deal with that kind of stuff sometimes in my line of business. Not often, but some." Sam grabbed his suspenders. "I'm just glad I can be of help. I can't believe someone is trying to get your pharmacy in trouble with a person as kind as Lyle owning it."

"I can't say I understand it myself." Holly jotted down the last of the information. "But I'm glad things are looking up." She handed him two pharmacy business cards with Lyle's name, pharmacy address, and phone number on them. "We need the sealed, signed letter soon. Okay?"

"I should be able to have that done in a few days and in the mail. We even have a notary who often visits our work site."

"Perfect, Sam. I can't thank you enough. Lyle will be so relieved. I know I am."

Holly and Josh shook Sam's hand, wishing him well. Holly had managed to keep her excitement tamped down so that she behaved professionally. But once they exited the trailer, her excitement ricocheted wildly inside her. As they made their way across the gravel parking lot toward the side of the trailer, each step she took was bouncier than the one before.

When Sam could no longer see them out the front window, even if he had been looking, and it seemed clear no one was aware of them, she turned to Josh. "I can't believe we did it! Finally!" She leaped in the air, and Josh caught her as if they were choreographed dancers.

He spun her around, grinning. After one spin he seemed to be embarrassed and set her down and straightened his shirt, regaining composure. "You did great. Everyone will be very proud of you."

"You absolutely know I could not have done it without your help." She was used to going alone when she traveled to Amish homes for her work, but it felt really nice to have a helper and a friend. She looked at Josh's slightly red face as he tried to avert his eyes from hers, even with a smile lingering on his face. She had told him that she wasn't available ever, and he was trying to respect that.

Could she follow through on staying single forever? Even if it meant losing Josh?

23

*B*randon pulled his phone out of his pocket, hit the email icon, and then hit Refresh. Nothing. It'd been thirteen days since he took his exams. He had done this at least twenty times today, and it was not quite ten in the morning. At any moment he could get the news about whether he passed or failed the pharmacist licensing and law exams. It took passing two exams to earn a license—the NAPLEX, which was the pharmacy competency and knowledge test, and the MPJE, which had federal- and state-specific questions about the laws that governed the industry. And with passing those tests would come the most precious series of numbers he could imagine: his pharmacist license.

Combine that with the vital information Holly had learned about what had actually happened on October fifteenth, and he would have the winning ticket to save his dad's pharmacy. But if he didn't pass one or both exams, it wasn't a complete loss. They now had enough information to clear Greene's Pharmacy. They just didn't have a pharmacist to take over Todd's hours, and they couldn't confront him until they hired someone to replace him.

"I've got this, man." Todd was working at the adjacent station, going through the morning prep. "Take a short break before we open. Usually the tech or intern doesn't have to show up until the customers are actually here."

"No, I'm fine." Brandon slid his phone back into his pocket and continued inputting into the computer the information from the faxes they had received overnight. There was no way he would take a break without Holly present, and Holly should start her shift any minute.

The front door opened and closed with a jingle from the multiple Christmas bells that now covered it. Holly was back from her morning deliveries with a few minutes to spare before opening time. Keeping Todd in his peripheral vision, he exited the gated prescription area and walked toward her.

"Good morning." She greeted him while simultaneously turning the sign on the front door to Open. "Any news about your exams?"

"Not yet, I'm afraid." He took another deep breath and tried to suppress his rising anxiety. He had dealt with minor test anxiety throughout his school career and had been increasingly more successful keeping it at bay over the past few years. But so much was riding on the results of these exams.

She touched his elbow and looked in his eyes. "Soon." She moved to one side of the front display and turned on a power strip. Lights on the Christmas tree immediately illuminated the store walls and window in a rainbow of colors. The animatronic snowman whirred to life, waving to passing people in the downtown area.

"You should tell your sister that this is quite the Christmas display. I don't think it's been this elaborate in previous years."

"Ya, she adds more every year. Eventually you'll be filling prescriptions next to live reindeer."

Brandon laughed at the thought and then stopped when he realized it didn't sound so bad to be filling scripts here in future Christmases.

Holly moved to the other side of the display windows and plugged in another power strip, starting the miniature train set, which took up the entire left window, in motion. When children arrived with their parents to shop, they could even use a control to make the train start and stop. Ivy had fashioned the set to vaguely resemble Raysburg, complete with tiny Amish buggies, farm houses set in miniature hills, and lots of animal figurines. In the very center was a nativity scene. Even when Brandon was working back in the prescription area, he had heard a lot of oohs and aahs from customers.

Holly peered past him for a moment, clearly checking on Todd's whereabouts. "I ran into the mail delivery lady on my way in. She was running ahead of schedule since she has extra helpers to deliver the Christmas packages. This came in the mail." Holly reached in her dress pocket, removed a white envelope, and handed it to Brandon. It was addressed to Lyle from Sam Miller and sealed with a notary stamp.

No doubt this was Sam's personal account of what had happened. It'd arrived in plenty of time before the board meeting, which Brandon had been concerned about. They also had Sam's full contact information—the name and NPI number of his doctor and the official five prescriptions transferred from Sam's home pharmacy—stored in paper format in a file in a safe Todd didn't have access to. That info and the letter Sam had sent would be more than enough evidence for the pharmacy to clear the charges against them.

"Wow, that was quick. You found him Monday, and today is only Friday." He kept his voice down so Todd couldn't hear what they were saying. "I'm so glad he agreed to help."

Holly nodded. "He was very agreeable. Most of our patients are incredibly grateful for what your dad does. They need him, and they need Greene's—if not for themselves, then for someone they love."

And Greene's needs me here. The thought hit hard, and he wasn't sure how he felt about it.

"Yes, they do," Brandon agreed. He pulled out his phone again and hit Refresh on the email. The circle spun, indicating the phone was receiving new data. It dinged softly as a new email arrived in his box. Brandon felt an immediate surge of adrenaline as he saw that the email was from the Pennsylvania State Board of Pharmacy. His heart seemed to race and stall simultaneously. He clicked, opening it, and skimmed for the important words.

Brandon Greene. Congratulations. Passed. License number.

He almost fell over with relief. Dozens of memories flashed through his mind as he stared at the email. Struggling through undergrad while grieving his mother's untimely death. All-night study sessions with fellow pharmacy school students. The heartbreak of a bad test score. Failing a class his first year and having to retake it in the summer. The embarrassment of counselors telling him he was unlikely to make it to graduation. The triumph of making an A in a class that was almost impossible. Hearing about the remaining classmates graduating without him. Hugging his father in Greene's storage room and finally forgiving him for everything that had happened to create the distance between them. In this moment it had all paid off.

"Brandon? Is everything okay?" Holly peered at him over his phone.

Brandon put the device in his pocket. "Yes. Yes, more than okay. I passed."

She grabbed his arm. "Congrats," she whispered.

"Thanks, Holly. I'm going upstairs to get Dad. We need to have a talk with Todd."

Fifteen minutes later Brandon was helping his father down the stairs, though the older man was trying to shrug off his help. Some things would never change. He'd gently told his dad what the security footage showed Todd doing, and Brandon had taken time to encourage his dad to sip water and take relaxing breaths as he absorbed the news. Once his heart rate had slowed to an almost normal rate, they'd headed down the steps.

"Dad, you stay calm and let me confront Todd." Brandon opened the door from the apartment stairs to the pharmacy.

"I'll try. But I have some things to say too." His father's voice was low and intense.

Maybe it would be good for his dad's health in the long run to look Todd in the eyes and say a few things.

"Todd, my father and I need to have a word with you in the break room."

He looked up from the computer with a start. Holly was working next to him, keeping the agreement that they would not let Todd out of their sight when he was in the pharmacy.

Had Todd's face turned pale? He had to know he was caught. "Oh, um, sure."

The three of them stepped into the break room, and Brandon closed the door behind them just in case any customers came into the store.

"Sit down." Brandon gestured at one chair while pulling up another for his dad. Todd sat across the table from Brandon and his dad and was now visibly sweating.

"Look, I don't know what this is about, but whatever you think happened, I'm sure it's a misunderstanding—"

"Just stop." Brandon held his hand up. "We know everything. You didn't realize it, but we'd paid a private security company to set up cameras and record footage here, which was stored off-site. So even though you thought you were off camera, you weren't. We saw you destroy the note my father wrote about transferring the prescriptions for Sam Miller, and we saw you shred the hard copies. I have undeniable digital proof that I will show to the Board of Pharmacy."

The remaining bit of color in Todd's face drained, even from his lips. He'd lose his license over this. Even if he didn't lose it permanently, his career was over. Who would hire someone that had sabotaged his employer? That used an older man's stroke in order to get an advantage? After this came out BB Drugs couldn't afford to keep him on even as a pharmacy tech. It would be really bad publicity for them.

Brandon laced his fingers together. "We also found Sam Miller and have all the information we need about his condition and his prescriptions to prove that the prescriptions were an emergency fill and were legitimate. We'll ask the board to bring charges against you for sabotage and false accusations. They don't take these things lightly. But before I possibly call the police to escort you out of here, what I really want to know is why. Why on earth would you do these things? I trusted you. I counted you as a family friend."

Todd scoffed. "Trust. Yeah, right." He drummed his fingers on the table. "If he"—Todd pointed to Dad—"had just trusted me years ago, we wouldn't be having this conversation now. The pharmacy would be making real profits, and you would have a family business you could actually be proud of. I spent time, oh so much time, learning how to modernize this place. I figured out numerous ways that would make a huge difference in Greene's profits. I wanted to be his partner and help this place grow! But he chose to operate a charity instead. That's no way to do business."

"It was never your business." Dad's voice was quiet but intense. "And because I knew you thought about money above all else, I could never take you on as a partner. I should have stood up and told my son no when he hired you, but I wanted to forgive, the way my Amish friends do. I wanted to believe you were here to help me during my time of need."

"I was trying to help you," Todd snapped. "It may not make sense to you, but if you had been fined by the board, you would sell. You'd have no other option. BB Drugs would have bought this place, and you could have retired comfortably. And, yeah, I could have gotten a bonus for opening a new location in this area. Why do you want to hold on to a dying model of business?"

His dad's eyes bore into Todd. "How I choose to run *my* business is none of your business. And you will not force me into retirement, a comfortable one or otherwise. Who do you think you are anyway?"

"I could've turned this place into a mega success, and there's still time to—"

"That's enough." Brandon leaned in, placing his palms on the table. "Your plan failed, and Dad isn't going anywhere. Neither is Greene's Pharmacy."

"Brandon, you're reasonable. Surely you can't intend to actually work here after you get your license. Talk with your dad." Todd wore a smile that looked forced. "We can still work out this deal. You all need me—and this chance."

"There is no deal. I am licensed now, and I will take over for my dad as pharmacist-in-charge until he is well enough to work again. And he will be soon. We will send the information we've uncovered to the board, and you can answer to them. But at the moment you can either calmly walk out with me right now, or I will call the police, and they will escort you."

Todd opened and closed his mouth several times as if he had more to say. "Fine. I'll leave." He made a hand motion as if tossing money. "Bankrupt yourselves. Good luck with this money pit." He stood and stormed out of the room. Brandon followed closely behind in case Todd tried to do anything stupid on his way out. Thankfully, words were the only thing he threw as he mumbled about how stupid Brandon was to root himself in this failing pharmacy. Todd walked out the front door and slammed it behind him, the numerous Christmas decorations reverberating from the impact.

Brandon let out a breath he hadn't realized he'd been holding. He looked over his shoulder to see Dad close behind him and Holly watching the whole thing from behind the counter.

Several customers left an aisle to see what was going on, and Brandon was at a loss to know how to handle the situation.

Dad waved at them. "What can I help you find today?"

Brandon didn't hover close enough to hear the whole conversation, but they seemed to relax, and within a minute they were laughing with his dad. When they returned to their browsing, Dad walked over to stand next to Brandon at the front door.

"I'm sorry, Dad." He looked down at the dark wood floor, watching the Christmas lights dance in the reflection. "I didn't know about what had happened between you and Todd. I should have trusted your opinion. I was just desperate for an easy solution so that when I got my license, I could leave, knowing Todd would be here until you were able to work full time again."

"It's not your fault." Dad patted his shoulder. "I should have told you. I was just hopeful that the issues between Todd and me were in the distant past." He walked back toward the pharmacy counter, and Brandon walked with him. "Now"—Dad tapped his hands against the counter—"I think some celebrating is in order. Let me take you and Holly out to dinner tonight. I'd say let's go now, but you have a workday ahead of you, Dr. Greene." Dad's eyes radiated pride. "Congratulations, you are officially more educated than I am."

Brandon laughed. "Hardly. A degree is great, but it doesn't replace years of hands-on experience in the trenches."

"Thank you, Son." Dad clasped Brandon's shoulder. "I feel guilty for having asked for your time. As of today, you could be earning real money with your degree and license. Can't tell you how much I'm grateful for it. But soon enough we can hire someone else, and you can be off."

"Please don't feel guilty. Apparently, and brace yourself for this, there are things more important than making money. You've spent my whole life trying to teach me that, and I get it now."

Dad's eyes misted.

"We can figure out how to handle the payments on my student loans, and I will stay as long as you need me. There will always be corporate jobs. What you, Holly, and Julie do for this community matters."

The bells on the front door jingled as a mother with a young child entered the store. When the little girl saw the train, she squealed with excitement. Her mother lingered near the train for a bit, embracing the girl's delight with the decorations, and then the woman moved to a nearby row of over-the-counter medications.

Holly pointed to the prescription work area. "Looks like we better get to work, Dr. Greene."

24

*S*now flurries tickled Holly's face as she walked down the sidewalk, and the view had her grinning ear to ear. She adjusted her scarf and black coat against the wind. No amount of cold weather could dampen her spirits today—a mere five days before Christmas. Booths of Amish-made Christmas gifts lined the sidewalks in front of the pharmacy. Raysburg sparkled with Christmas lights, decorations, and falling snow. The delicious fragrance of hot apple pies swirled from the booth next to her, and her mouth watered in response.

"Guder Marye, Fannie," she greeted her Mamm's good friend and vendor of the pie booth. The pies were wrapped in tinfoil inside a gas-powered warmer.

"Hallo, Holly Noelle." Fannie beamed at her, the skin around her eyes crinkling so much they almost disappeared. "Care for a fry pie? No charge for you, of course. I have apple, chocolate, caramel, and blueberry."

Holly started to politely decline, as she usually was too busy to stop and enjoy something like dessert at eleven o'clock on a Wednesday morning, but she stopped herself. "You know what? Sure. How about apple?"

Fannie, still smiling, handed her the pie, along with several paper towels. Holly took it with her gloved hands. The steamy warmth of the dessert came through the cloth, and she cupped it closer, inhaling it.

"Denki, Fannie."

"No." Fannie's eyes brimmed with tears, and her voice broke. "Denki to *du,* Holly, and you know why."

Holly stood there, fully aware of what Fannie meant, and allowed the woman's gratitude to surround her like a warm feather comforter on a cold winter night. Holly had convinced Fannie's husband, Vernon, to let Holly take him to see a doctor, but it hadn't been easy. She'd navigated all his arguments while gently and firmly insisting he go with her to have a slow-healing cut on his leg tended to. After everything was said and done—which included a week of home health-care visits while Vernon was attached to an IV with antibiotics and then a month of oral antibiotics—the doctor told them if he'd waited one more day, he probably would've lost his leg, maybe his life. Fannie wiped her eyes. "With all of us being here today, surely we can raise enough money for you to have another health fair."

Joy welled in Holly's chest, and she wanted to respond with honesty and gratitude that God had given her the wisdom to convince Vernon of what needed to be done. But all Holly could manage was a nod and a faint smile. She glanced down the street, taking in the Christmas spirit of people sacrificing for one another. Multiple booths had steaming foods perfect for cold weather. Other decorated stalls had beautiful handmade Christmas goods. Finally her composure returned. "If the busyness is any indication, it looks as if we'll raise plenty for another health fair, plus some to put aside for future years."

"Have you seen the section of the craft fair inside the empty shop?"

"Nee." Holly looked two doors down from the pharmacy and saw clean windows where there had been murky ones. How much work had her people and the Englisch put into this event? "I was going to head that way now." She took a bite of her pie as she waved to Fannie. "Bye," she mumbled around the crispy shell and gooey filling. It did not disappoint. She licked her lips as she continued down the sidewalk. When she passed the pharmacy entrance, her sister's over-the-top Christmas decorations were in the display windows, and someone was playing with the train set. Brandon was working in the pharmacy along with their backup tech, Sandy. Holly hoped they had enough staffing for the increased foot traffic the craft fair was generating, but Brandon and Lyle insisted she take the day off, walk around, and enjoy it.

"Hey there, Sis." A slender arm snaked inside the crook of her elbow, and Ivy grinned, holding her own pie wrapped in tinfoil. "What do you think of all this?"

"It's just amazing." When her mom was planning the craft market-place, Holly had hoped it could earn some money to go toward another health fair, but this was beyond what she'd imagined. The community had sacrificed so much during this busy time of year in order to help her. She couldn't remember a time that she had felt so empowered and supported.

"Come on." Ivy tugged at Holly's arm. "I'll show you what we have set up in the empty store. I was able to talk the building's owner into let-ting us use it today for free."

Holly let her sister lead her along the downtown street. They waved at the vendors, all women they had known personally for most of their lives. Another family friend handed each sister a cup of steaming hot cof-fee as they passed. Englisch shoppers mingled with Amish to look at the various goods and foods.

A large rectangular yellow vehicle caught Holly's attention as it parked across the way. "Is that a field trip bus?" Holly's question seemed silly the moment the bus doors opened and a line of elementary-aged children began streaming out. "Do public schools still have class this time of year?"

"One of the districts is in session until the twenty-third this year." Ivy shrugged. "Don't know why. I appealed to some schoolteacher friends that Mamm and I occasionally clean for. They were able to convince their school to let them take their classes to our market, a 'multicultural' activity, I believe. Lots of the children will get a good opportunity to purchase a special Christmas surprise for their mom or dad."

What a treat for the children and for this benefit. "Have I told you lately, Ivy, that you're brilliant?"

"No, but you don't have to. I'm fully aware." Ivy tilted her chin and stuck out the tip of her tongue, making the silly face she'd made since childhood. "Now, come on and let's go inside. It's cold out here away from the heaters."

Holly chuckled. For someone so passionate about all things Christmas, Ivy had quite a dislike of cold weather. When Ivy opened the door, bells jingled in the entrance of the usually empty shop. Lines of tables filled the center of the building. One section was fashioned into a toy shop, with Amish faceless dolls, wooden trains and buggies, rocking horses, red wagons, and several other items that Holly would have to inspect closer to see. Another area had assorted wall decorations and signs, some Christmas themed and some meant for any time of the year. Gorgeous, vibrantly colored quilts hung on the walls.

"Wow," Holly whispered. "Who would've thought the normally drab building could be transformed into this?"

"I know." Ivy's beautiful eyes glimmered. "You deserve all the effort it took to put this together, Holly. I'm going to help Mamm with her sign booth. Red called yesterday. You remember him?" Ivy's mouth curved into that telltale sign of teasing. "Our baby brother said he was trying to be here for the market, but it could be as late as Christmas Eve. Come see us in a bit. But for now I think I see someone who wants to talk to you." Ivy nodded at something behind Holly.

Holly turned. Josh Smucker . . . standing right behind her. She jumped a bit in surprise.

"Sorry." He put a hand on her arm to steady her. "Didn't mean to sneak up on you." His cheeks reddened a bit.

"You sure about that?" Holly grinned at him.

"I'm sure, because if I'd done it on purpose, I'd have come better prepared for you throwing that hot drink in your hand all over me. Although it's not the worst thing I've had on me today. I do work with chickens after all."

"How are your babies?"

"Not babies anymore. I've heard this variety may lay their first eggs by the end of January, although they will be too small to sell at first. I think it's safe to say that the birds are big enough to survive this winter with minimal effort on my part. We have their coop winterized and an outdoor area for them to stretch their legs, supervised of course."

"Of course. Congrats, Papa."

Josh laughed. "I think you are the one who deserves to hear 'congrats.' This looks like a success already, and there's still most of the day left for people to shop."

"Ya, I have to say I'm a little surprised that this many people are volunteering their time."

"You shouldn't be." Josh's lips formed a handsome smile.

Warmth spread through her, and she knew it wasn't just because of the cozy displays, heated room, or large crowd. It was love. Love for her community accepting her for who she was, including her health-care mission. She was willing to push cultural boundaries to get her message across: health care is vital and important, even for the Amish. But it was quite a wonderful gift to have support and be appreciated. And if she was truly accepted in this regard, was Ivy right about the community being open to her continuing her work *and* possibly having a husband and family of her own?

She looked into Josh's deep-brown eyes, marveling at the light that shone behind them. Was she willing to open herself up to a relationship after all? Her heart raced at the thought.

Brandon handed the prescription bag to the Amish teenager in front of him. "Glad Julie could fit you in while you were in town today for the market. An ear infection can be really painful if left untreated. This should clear it up though, and quickly. You'll be feeling much better by Christmas. Take one tablet twice a day for ten days, and remember to keep taking it even if you feel better."

"Thank you so much, Doc."

"You can just call me Brandon. I put the charge on your parents' tab. Don't worry. It's only a few dollars. Remember, you can call or stop by the pharmacy if you have any questions or need anything else. We'll be closed only on Christmas Eve and Christmas Day."

"Thanks again." The young man walked away from the counter, clutching the bag with the antibiotic that would ease the pain in his ear. He waved at Julie as she and Nacho entered the store and walked toward the prescription counter. She smiled at her patient as he passed and then at Brandon.

"Hey there, Dr. Greene." She leaned against the counter. Nacho sat, his big pink tongue lolling in a doggy smile.

"Ha. Yes, everyone keeps making that joke even though I don't know any more today than I did two weeks ago before I officially got my license."

"Well, we are all excited for you. I brought you some food. You know, again." She waved a brown paper bag in the air. "Figured you wouldn't get to close for lunch with all the increased foot traffic from the craft market."

"Yeah, I was planning to work through lunch and just eat a protein bar. It's already midday, and we close in only a few more hours anyway." His stomach growled at the mention of food. "Thank you. You didn't have to bring me anything. I know it's a workday for you too."

"I'm on break and stretching our legs." She rubbed Nacho on the top of his head. "Plus, I'm taking advantage of the limited time I have to bring you meals."

Brandon laughed. "Surely you have someone better to feed."

She shrugged. "Eh, not really, no. Other than my Amish friends, my boss, your father, and this big fella." She scratched the yellow Lab behind an ear. "I pretty much just hang out with myself here in town. Sometimes I make trips to visit friends on my days off. Not that I mind living in Raysburg. Still, I'll miss our chats when you leave town. Your dad seems to be doing better, and now that you have your license, I imagine you have another job lined up."

"Well, no. I did have an offer from BB Drugs, but I ended up declining it." He cleaned up a few stray pens from around the register and placed them in their cup.

Jules angled her head. "Wasn't that your whole goal? Get done, move away, make money?"

"I thought it was." Brandon raised a shoulder. "I assumed I'd be working in Philadelphia with my girlfriend by the New Year. But that wasn't the right fit for me, and neither was she. We ended things last month. And I'm staying here at Greene's for as long as my dad needs a pharmacist to run the place. I couldn't see trusting it to anyone else."

"I'm sorry. About the breakup, not about your staying." She paused, looking unsure of what to say. "I went through a bad breakup right before I moved out here. That's hard."

"It's okay. Some relationships don't work out, and that's just part of life."

"Oh, agreed. Also I heard about what your relief pharmacist did, and I'm sorry to hear about that too. How horrible."

"Yeah, that was rough, but thankfully it's all squared away, and we can put it in the past. The pharmacy board sided with us, as I knew they would after we had the evidence we needed. They dropped all charges against us, and they are filing charges against Todd for false claims and sabotage."

"The dropped charges against Greene's is a huge relief for everyone."

"Absolutely." Brandon drew a deep breath and rubbed his chest as he released it. "Wholeheartedly." Brandon glanced behind him at his workstation. "I'd offer for you to come behind the counter and have a seat with me as we eat lunch, but that's not technically legal. And I need to stay in the pharmacy so we can keep it open."

"Oh really? So you are worried about my trustworthiness around the important medications . . . many of which I prescribed?"

"Obviously." Brandon winked at her. "Of course there's always the option of you getting registered as a tech so you can come back and hang out with me. And your beast of course. First doggy pharmacy tech in the state. But that could take a while, so why don't we go to dinner tonight?"

Jules narrowed her eyes at him. "That was a pretty smooth transition, Brandon Greene."

"I do try. But in all seriousness I like talking to you and hanging out with you. You helped sell Raysburg to me as a place I can actually enjoy. It doesn't have to be a serious date or anything. Just sustenance and conversation."

"That would be wonderful."

25

*F*all on your knees! O hear the angel voices! O night divine, O night when Christ was born!"

Joshua lifted his voice to join the other carolers. All of them were assembled on a small hill overlooking the frozen pond. Golden evening light shimmered on the snow as the sun moved toward the horizon. About fifty people, both singles and some of their families, were gathered either on or around the icy pond. He liked this Amish tradition of gathering on a pond to skate, and Ivy's plan to have carolers here on Christmas Eve made it even better.

"O night, O holy night, O night divine!"

They wrapped up the song, the harmonies ringing like bells across the hard surface of the frozen water. Fresh snow had fallen the night before, but some men had cleared it from the pond and smoothed the surface before the evening's events in preparation for ice-skating. The bonfire, which was just getting started when they began singing, was now burning brightly.

"That was wonderful, everyone!" Ivy clapped her mitten-clad hands together. "Merry Christmas! Go enjoy it." She waved at everyone as their group started to disperse.

Roy, another caroler, clapped Joshua's shoulder. "Glad you could come and sing with us this year, Joshua."

"Ya, it was good to come make some music." Despite the practices being tinged with disappointment, Joshua had enjoyed it. He would miss the social time that singing with this group brought, although it wasn't really feasible for him to continue commuting this far without the opportunity to court Holly.

As the other singers dispersed, Joshua went toward the fire and spotted a familiar face looking right at him.

"Hallo." Holly smiled, her hands in black mittens clasped in front of her. She had on a black wool coat and scarf, with her black bonnet for warmth. Her nose and cheeks were slightly pink from the cold, which Joshua found adorable. "The singing was lovely."

"Glad you enjoyed the carols." Joshua found it difficult and slightly painful to keep seeing her, knowing she'd never be available for a relationship, but it was worth the pain to be near her. How could he justify continuing to see her now that they had cleared the pharmacy's name and he had finished his commitment of caroling?

"Would you"—she looked down at her mittens, seeming as if she was nervous—"want to, uh, take a walk?"

"Sure. Mind if we walk toward that warm fire, though? I hear there are s'mores to be had."

"Ya, that would be wonderful. But first I need to, um, talk with you before we get surrounded by people."

Joshua could feel himself frowning at her, but he couldn't seem to relax his face. What could she need to say? Was she going to tell him that she couldn't remain friends with him either? Surely that couldn't be it. Nevertheless, he nodded. "Okay, how about that bridge over the frozen stream?"

Without responding to his question, she headed that way. They walked through the snow, and with each step Joshua felt more nervous. What was going on that she needed to talk in private?

Once she reached the middle of the footbridge, she stopped and turned toward him. "I've been thinking a lot about my life and my Daed over the past few weeks." She cleared her throat. "You would have liked him. He was pretty passionate about dairy cows—the way you are about your chickens—treating them right even if it required more work. But more than that, he was passionate about my Mamm. They were so in love." She looked out over the landscape, lips upturned and shaking her head at what he assumed was some memory. "Every year at this time he would keep a sprig of plastic mistletoe in his pocket so he could hold it over her head and get extra kisses throughout the day. She would roll her eyes, but she always gave in."

Joshua offered a small smile, knowing it had to be painful to talk about her father. "Sounds a bit like my parents. They used to embarrass me so badly when I was younger." They leaned against the handrail, overlooking what in warmer months was a little tributary feeding into the lake. The sun was setting through the bare trees of the hills. Was this what she'd wanted, to simply talk to a friend about the heartaches she still carried? "I'm sorry for your loss, Holly."

"Oh, uh, no, what I mean is they embraced their life together, even in the simple day-to-day things. As sad as it is that he died too young, it would have been worse if he'd never truly lived. And he lived each day with my Mamm to the fullest. And . . . I . . . I want that too."

His breath caught in his throat. Was she really saying what he thought she was?

She pushed against the handrail and stood straight. "I know I've put you through a lot. I've confused you and hurt your feelings on multiple occasions. And maybe I'm jumping way ahead, but it's how my mind works."

"You aren't willing to take a first step down a path if you'll have to stop and backtrack. I get that. It's a bit challenging but definitely admirable."

"I'm glad you feel that way because I've been thinking about the bishop, and it seems that if we talked to him with humility and respect, he would rethink his stance. It might take a bit of patience and listening as he preaches his advice, but I want to try if you'll still have me." She looked up at him, and he could see all the nervousness and vulnerability displayed in her clear blue eyes. "Am I assuming too much?"

His insides were jumping for joy. "Absolutely not."

"Good. Because I'm in love with you."

Was this real? His heart leaped. "Best Christmas ever." He cupped her face with his hand, cherishing the feel of her soft, warm cheeks. He bent and captured her lips with his. Time seemed to both slow and speed up, and when they parted, their breaths were short and fast, visible in the chilly air.

"I'm in love with you too, Holly. But I think I've been pretty obvious about that."

"Ya," she whispered. "But it's good to hear it out loud."

He laughed, and the tension inside him disappeared. It was as if a fire were burning inside his heart, warming him more than any bonfire could. He removed one of her mittens and drew her hand to his lips. "If you think your bishop will listen, I believe you. Is it possible that next year we could have a Christmas wedding?"

"Wow, you move fast." But she was smiling, staring at the hand he'd kissed, which was still close to his lips.

He supposed it was unusual to leap into marriage talk so soon, even for people raised as they were. And he was sure he had a goofy-looking smile on his face as he asked the question. But he had never been considered smooth, and it wasn't as if he was going to start fooling her now. She apparently liked him for who he was.

"I can't help it." He lowered her hand from his lips and squeezed it. "There will never be anyone else I feel this way about."

Holly turned to face the sunset, still holding his hand. "Me neither." She leaned her head against his shoulder. "It won't be easy, you know, navigating a life with me."

He kissed the top of her black winter bonnet. "Easy is overrated. I never wanted easy. I want you. And any amount of time with you would be worth whatever it takes, plus more."

26

olly's mind zipped and zinged with new thoughts about family life and love and duty. Josh gently squeezed her hand from across the back seat of his driver's small sedan. The white Christmas lights of Raysburg twinkled as they drove through the downtown area.

"You okay?" he whispered.

Hope for their future continued to warm her, but all she managed in response to his question was a nod. "You?"

"Yeah, just still recovering from the wild swarm of Smuckers."

She laughed. "Ya, me too. I'm glad I met them, though."

Second Christmas had been amazing. She'd met all the Smucker siblings and their families at Josh's house. Her family's Christmas Day with Mamm, Ivy, Red, and herself had been a calm and quiet one. But with the big gathering of Josh's siblings, their spouses, nieces, nephews, and a few aunts and uncles, more than seventy-five people had been inside that home, and it'd been really loud and busy. No wonder Josh had grown to be a quiet person. It was hard to get a word in edgewise . . . unless one was put on the spot with a gazillion questions, as she had been. But the family's love was even bigger than the noise.

"I was afraid my family would scare you off."

She patted his hand. "Nee, you can't get rid of me that easily."

He lifted her hand to his lips and kissed it. "Now that's worth celebrating."

After the family gathering Josh had hired a driver to take them to Greene's. When the pharmacy closed at seven, Lyle was having a small party to celebrate Christmas and their victory in finding Sam Miller. There just hadn't been time to fit in an office party before Christmas.

The driver, George, pulled into a parking space a half block from Greene's. Although today was a holiday for the Amish, there were lots of Englischers downtown, shopping bags in hand. Were many stores other than Greene's staying open until seven o'clock on the day after Christmas? Apparently so. The driver waved at them as they exited the car.

They went toward the store, and she noticed Julie and Nacho walking toward them on the sidewalk, probably also headed to Greene's for the "day-late Christmas party."

"Merry Christmas!" Holly waved.

Julie looked up, seeming surprised. "Well, hello, you two turtledoves."

Josh scratched his head near his black felt hat. "Turtledoves?"

Julie grinned while closing the gap between them. "You know, like the song?"

Holly laughed. She knew it well. "The Twelve Days of Christmas" would often play in the pharmacy during the month of December. She reached down to pet Nacho when he was close enough. "Is Nacho the partridge in the pear tree?"

Julie pointed at the pharmacy. "Hmm, maybe Lyle's the partridge, and the pharmacy is the pear tree."

Holly grinned. "Let's go have a party at the pear tree then."

The red-painted door with its decorated wreath welcomed them. She'd never take this place for granted. *Denki*. She sent up a silent prayer of thanks to God for their success in finding Sam and for Lyle's improving health.

Josh opened the door and held it for her. "Happy birthday, Holly," he whispered as she passed him.

"Surprise!" An array of voices, including her brother's, chorused in unison.

Holly laughed. "Denki!" She stepped inside. Her little brother had arrived on Christmas Eve, but he'd return to his place and his job in a couple of days.

There were two folding tables decorated with Christmas-themed tablecloths, bowls of nuts and fruit, and a large, colorful cake.

Birthday? It was technically her birthday, but she didn't think they were celebrating that.

Pop! Confetti and streamers shot around her, and she looked up to see Ivy holding a confetti cannon.

"Ivy." Mamm had a chiding tone, but she was smiling.

Ivy put her hands in the air. "Don't worry. I will vacuum it all up." She shrugged. "*After* the party."

Lyle stepped forward and gave her a hug. "Happy birthday, kiddo."

"Thank you," Holly whispered and squeezed him tight. She released him, ready to greet the next person closest to her.

Brandon put an arm around her shoulders. "I absolutely do not know what we'd do without you, Holly Noelle—not on a business or personal level."

She leaned into his hug. "The feeling is mutual." She didn't know what she'd do without any of them. But thankfully they were a part of her, and she looked forward to the coming years . . . decades . . . and lifetime.

The party was lively, and everyone mingled and ate and played games for more than an hour before some began to leave. Most everyone here had worked all day, and they were wiped out from yesterday being Christmas Day and all the busyness that had led up to it. But how fun that everyone found the energy to be here tonight. She and Josh stood together near the doorway, bidding dear friends and family goodbye. Lyle, Julie, Brandon, and Holly's family remained—the cleanup crew, she guessed.

Ivy held out Holly's coat. "Put it on and get out, you and Josh both. We've got this." Ivy shoved Josh's coat into his chest. "Take a walk, Sis. When you're ready for a romantic carriage ride, Mamm parked ours in the Martel Clinic lot. Lyle will drive us home when we're done here."

"But—" Holly shook her head and glanced at Josh.

"She's right, Holly Noelle." Lyle kissed her cheek. "Get."

Ivy opened the door and basically shoved them out, laughing before she winked.

When Holly stumbled onto the sidewalk, giggling, Josh steadied her. A gust of cold wind chilled her, feeling like icy fingers down her neck. Snow flurries were blowing by, and the scent of snow on asphalt was in the frigid breeze. She pulled her coat tighter around her. "Brr."

Josh unwrapped his scarf from his coat collar, draped it around her neck, and tied it.

Holly gazed up at him. "Oh, that's much better. Denki."

He smiled and kissed her forehead before holding out his hand for hers.

She took his hand, and they walked down the sidewalk. His scarf smelled like him, and she was so grateful they were together. How had she convinced herself that it was her duty to remain single for her entire life? That hadn't felt at all difficult or lonely until she met Josh.

The streetlamps and the many strands of Christmas lights illuminated their steps, making the walk easy even though it was nighttime.

He leaned in. "Tell me your thoughts on marriage, Holly Noelle."

She stopped short, blinking.

"Kumm on. We're in love, but how did you jump from running to professing your love?"

She took a deep breath. "Fair question." She started walking again, gathering her thoughts.

Josh inclined his head. "I'm listening."

She nodded. "Well, first you need to know that the bishop and his wife dropped by the house yesterday, bringing us freshly baked coffee cake, and I dared to ask how he might feel about me getting married one day. He grew serious and asked if the young man was Amish. When I said your name, he grinned and nodded and said the three of us needed to talk about it."

"That's great. And I meant it when I said I didn't want to change you. I don't expect you to give up something that's a huge part of who you are, and I wouldn't want you to."

She never dreamed she'd find an Amish man who had such a view on women and marriage. "Denki."

"All that leaves as an obstacle is my bishop. But if your bishop approves us getting married, I feel mine will adjust after a few conversations. We need his approval to live in my district after we marry, but we have a great situation for a family with a working mom. Since I run the farm and my parents live here, someone will always be home. It's a house filled with love. And a farm filled with chickens. And what child wouldn't want to have chickens? I know I loved it."

"Ya." She grinned. "Ya, that all sounds wonderful, including the chickens. Your family, including all the relatives I met today, really enjoy each other. They don't fret over messes or work that needs to be done. They really treasure each moment, you know?"

"Yep, although each one is a really loud moment. I'd say you'll get used to it, but I don't know if that's true, because I'm not sure I am."

She lightly elbowed him in the ribs.

"But, Holly, none of that tells me how your opinion about marriage went from staunchly reluctant to willingly ready."

"Ya, that's pretty hard to explain. I've done a lot of thinking and praying, and when one seeks answers, one finds them. A particular insight that really made a difference is the story of Mary and Martha. You know, where Martha is doing all the things she's supposed to do—cleaning, waiting on her guests, preparing food, but missing the point of Jesus's visit. And then there's Mary sitting at the feet of her Savior, not missing a moment. Your family feels like Mary. Soaking up all the love and trusting God that the rest will work itself out. But I tend to be more like Martha. I try to do all the things I think I'm supposed to do. But maybe God is calling me to have more of a Mary heart. Be in the present. Be here for love. Trust in Him that I can still help people in the way that I feel called *and* have a family with you."

"Wow. I'd say something deeper, but it's all I've got. Wow."

"Does that feel right to you too?"

"Definitely. I was thinking about a different Mary earlier today, the mother of Jesus. She was judged harshly for being pregnant outside of marriage, and you may be judged pretty harshly at times too when you go back to work a few months after a baby is born. But apparently God isn't nearly as concerned with how things appear as He is with us doing what He's called us to do."

She stopped short again. "Okay, my turn to say 'wow.' That's a really good insight. I'm going to hold on to it, and it's not like He'd lead me this far and abandon me."

"No, He never would. And while I'm not perfect like Him, I won't abandon you either. We'll find the right path for us and our family." He cradled her cheeks in his hands.

She stood on her toes to kiss him in the swirling flurries. Relief and joy at his acceptance filled her to the brim. Somehow they'd work things out. Even though she had reservations about what kind of wife and mother she'd be, he'd be there to balance her, encourage her, and strengthen her.

They drew the kiss to an end, and she rested her head on his chest as he held her.

She'd spend the rest of her days grateful that God saw her value and that He'd given her a like-minded lifetime partner who loved her for who she was.

Acknowledgments

To my (Cindy's) daughter-in-law and my (Erin's) sister-in-law, Shweta Woodsmall, PharmD—Thank you for giving us insight into the behind-the-scenes workings of an independent pharmacy.

To all the other members of our family—You encourage and strengthen us and make life interesting . . . and hectic!

To WaterBrook Multnomah, from editorial to marketing to sales to production—Thank you!

To Shannon Marchese, Executive Editor—You're still the one!

To Carol Bartley, line editor, fact checker, time-line keeper—You're amazing.

To Cindy from Erin—This was the first work we completed together, even though it was released later. I can't thank you enough for teaching me about writing and for letting me into your world of fiction. You're a treasure.

THE AMISH *of* SUMMER GROVE SERIES

Ariana's comfortable Old Order Amish world is about to unravel. Will holding tightly to the cords of family keep them together—or simply tear them apart?

 **WATERBROOK**